REA

P9-EEN-356

Did the woman ever take no for an answer?

She seemed pretty damned confident she could win his boys over in one morning. That in itself was enough for him to mark his territory. To say no. But what if the twins had a good time? What if they did make friends? What if Jared was stimulated enough to speak again? Could he deny them the opportunity?

"Okay," he agreed, torn between what was right for his boys and what he felt he could handle himself.

What felt right for him was minimal contact with this woman who didn't seem to know how to stay out of his personal space.

He couldn't shake the sensation that she'd taken his family on as a pet project.

And he didn't like it one bit.

ROMANCE

Dear Reader,

I'm a Virgo. Make that a stereotypical Virgo. A woman who makes lists and likes a tidy universe. When I feel things are spinning out of control and I wail, "I want my life back!" my husband always brings me down to earth by saying, "This is life, Amy." So I'm always fascinated by stories of people who are making other plans when life and love throw them a curve.

My hero, Gabriel, who desperately wants his life back, is so focused on his future that he doesn't recognize the comfort and joy Olivia is offering in the present. Not that Olivia doesn't have second thoughts. Hesitating to upset her ordered existence, she dismisses the intense attraction she feels for Gabriel as mere longing. Come on, guys, stand under the mistletoe and give love a chance! If you think you *always* get to choose the direction your life is taking, you're kidding yourselves and missing out on some really scenic detours…um, sorry…I seem to be channeling my husband. But I really do hope you, dear reader, will cheer Gabriel and Olivia on toward the happiness they could experience if they'd just get out of their own way and let life run its course.

All my best,

Amy

COMFORT AND JOY
Amy Frazier

HARLEQUIN®

TORONTO • NEW YORK • LONDON
AMSTERDAM • PARIS • SYDNEY • HAMBURG
STOCKHOLM • ATHENS • TOKYO • MILAN • MADRID
PRAGUE • WARSAW • BUDAPEST • AUCKLAND

If you purchased this book without a cover you should be aware that this book is stolen property. It was reported as "unsold and destroyed" to the publisher, and neither the author nor the publisher has received any payment for this "stripped book."

ISBN-13: 978-0-373-71456-8
ISBN-10:   0-373-71456-4

COMFORT AND JOY

Copyright © 2007 by Amy Lanz.

All rights reserved. Except for use in any review, the reproduction or utilization of this work in whole or in part in any form by any electronic, mechanical or other means, now known or hereafter invented, including xerography, photocopying and recording, or in any information storage or retrieval system, is forbidden without the written permission of the publisher, Harlequin Enterprises Limited, 225 Duncan Mill Road, Don Mills, Ontario, Canada M3B 3K9.

This is a work of fiction. Names, characters, places and incidents are either the product of the author's imagination or are used fictitiously, and any resemblance to actual persons, living or dead, business establishments, events or locales is entirely coincidental.

This edition published by arrangement with Harlequin Books S.A.

® and TM are trademarks of the publisher. Trademarks indicated with ® are registered in the United States Patent and Trademark Office, the Canadian Trade Marks Office and in other countries.

www.eHarlequin.com

Printed in U.S.A.

ABOUT THE AUTHOR

Having worked at various times as a teacher, a media specialist, a professional storyteller and a freelance artist, Amy Frazier now writes full-time. She lives in Georgia with her husband, two philosophical cats and one very rascally terrier-mix dog.

Books by Amy Frazier

HARLEQUIN SUPERROMANCE

Don't miss any of our special offers. Write to us at the following address for information on our newest releases.

Harlequin Reader Service
U.S.: 3010 Walden Ave., P.O. Box 1325, Buffalo, NY 14269
Canadian: P.O. Box 609, Fort Erie, Ont. L2A 5X3

PROLOGUE

JUST AS THE RISING SUN was clearing her windowsill, eight-year-old Olivia Marshall slipped out of bed. She didn't intend to waste a minute of the last day of summer vacation. The last day before the start of third grade. For her. Gabriel would be starting fifth grade. And as much fun as they'd had this vacation—thrown together by accident, or luck— Olivia knew fifth-grade boys didn't even acknowledge the existence of, let alone play with, third-grade girls. Tomorrow she was going to lose her best friend.

The birds were singing loudly as she pulled on shorts and a T-shirt. She didn't bother with shoes. Her stomach grumbled loudly, but she resisted the call of food. She needed to think of a goodbye present for Gabriel. Trailing her fingers over her bookshelves and desk, she tried to decide which of her treasures she could bear to part with.

The potato that looked like Mr. Hitchens from the dry cleaner's? No. Over the past couple of months the potato had shriveled and sprouted, and although it had once made the two of them hold their sides with laughter, now it didn't resemble anyone they knew. Olivia didn't throw it away, though. You never knew who or what it might begin to look like in the future.

How about her copy of King Arthur's adventures? She and Gabriel had spent hours sitting in the branches of the big old maple in her backyard, reading chapters and then acting them out. They both agreed knights and jousts and dragons and quests for the grail were as exciting as any of their favorite TV shows or comics. But the book was big, and Olivia couldn't see Gabriel carrying it around. His school friends might think he was a dork.

No, she wanted to give him something that he could keep in his pocket. Kind of like a secret. To remember this summer. To remember her. Because she was going to miss him so much.

He was the kind of person you wanted watching your back. As brave as the whole A-Team put together. As adventurous as Sally Ride. As loyal as a Yankees fan. As funny as *The Jeffersons*. And as cute—yeah, she had to admit he was cute—as Michael J. Fox.

Her gaze fell on the Indian Head penny that was her prize possession. She'd found it digging in the backyard B.G.—Before Gabriel—and the strong Indian profile was her idea of a real hero. She picked up the coin. It wouldn't be easy giving it up.

But it wasn't going to be easy giving up Gabriel's friendship, either.

This would be her gift. Dropping it into her pocket, she picked up a marker to cross off today's date on her calendar, as she did every morning. September 6, 1983. Then she raced downstairs to grab the granola she'd put in plastic bags the night before.

She and Gabriel were going to Shem Creek to build a dam and catch bullfrogs.

CHAPTER ONE

How MUCH PRIDE DID a man have to swallow to ensure his kids' well-being?

Gabriel Brant figured he was about to find out.

As he drove past a sign that read, Welcome to Hennings, Best Little City in New York State, he glanced in his rearview mirror to check on the twins. Justin's eyes—far too old for a five-year-old's—met his.

"Daddy, Jared's hungry." Ever since Hurricane Katrina had destroyed their home and Gabriel's restaurant a little over two years ago, Jared hadn't spoken. With the uncanny sensitivity of a twin, Justin spoke for him.

"We're almost at your grandfather's." The thought worked Gabriel's stomach into knots. "He said he'd have lunch ready." Something out of a can, more than likely. The old man would do it deliberately. To emphasize that a talent for cooking was no big deal.

A third of the way down Main Street, Gabriel turned right onto Chestnut, where the storefronts gave way to residences. Two days before Thanksgiving and still not a snowflake in sight, yet some of the houses were already decorated for Christmas.

"Daddy, we see Santa!" Justin exclaimed, pointing to a large plastic figure next to one front door. "Does he come to Grampa's, too?"

The twins could remember the motel, and then the cramped mobile home "city," in which they'd spent the past two Christmases. Where charities had provided a holiday chow line and a few presents for the kids.

Outsiders simply did not understand or want to understand how this particular storm had not gone away. Its devastating effects still lingered months and months and months afterward. The enormity of rebuilding and the inescapable red tape involved with the process kept countless lives in a state of perpetual uncertainty. Gabriel was sick and tired of waiting. Wanting a real roof over his boys' heads this holiday season was one of several compelling reasons he'd finally given in to Walter Brant's appeal to come home. Trouble was, Hennings hadn't felt like home to Gabriel for seventeen years.

"Does Santa come here, too?" Justin pressed.

"I believe he does." Gabriel would make sure he did, even though the money situation was stickier than gum on a New Orleans sidewalk.

He pulled into his father's driveway. Backed by lowering clouds, the squat brick Craftsman-style house with the broad front porch seemed to scowl at him. After the past two years, Gabriel had inured himself to feeling on the outs. Almost.

The return to Hennings galled him, sure, but his sons needed to be in a place that didn't automatically mistrust them, didn't patronize them because of their plight or refer to them as "refugees." As if their misfortune had been their fault.

Whether Gabriel liked it or not, Hennings was his hometown, and he had every right to return. Every right—no, he had an obligation—to give his twins a fresh start. Compared to the protracted chaos left in the wake of Katrina, Walter would be a balmy breeze.

Right.

"We're here," he said, trying to infuse the words with enthusiasm.

"You think Grampa will make po'boys for lunch?" Justin asked.

"I doubt it, kiddo. Until I can get to the store for supplies, you two will be eating…the Grampa Walter special. Which definitely won't be what you're used to. But you'll be real polite, y'hear?"

"Yessir. Polite as curtsyin' crawdads."

Gabriel smiled at the silly reply the last of a string of babysitters had taught the boys. She'd been nice. But like so many others, she'd left—out of necessity—for greener pastures. In her case, a sister's in Fort Worth.

Both boys unbuckled and clambered out of their booster seats as Gabriel opened the back door. But when Walter appeared on the front porch, Justin and Jared remained in the car. Gabriel hadn't told his sons much about their grandfather, because he wasn't sure of the reception they'd receive.

"Come on, you two. Let's go meet your grampa."

It was a short but frosty walk between the car and the porch, the November day only partially contributing to the chill.

"What took you so long?" Walter asked as they climbed the steps.

"Traffic," Gabriel replied.

"I mean what took you so long? Your rooms have been ready for two years now."

And so it began.

"You know I needed to stay close to New Orleans. To see if I'd be allowed to rebuild the restaurant." Into which he'd sunk every last dime of his savings. Lost every last dime was more like it, if the class-action insurance suit didn't pay off. "The powers that be haven't ruled on that yet."

"If you'd stayed in New York, you wouldn't have been in the path of that hurricane."

"Don't start."

The two men eyed each other in an antagonistic standoff.

"Well, am I gonna get a proper introduction?" Walter groused, looking down at the boys. "Five years old, and yet to meet their grampa. Kept away that long, you'd think these kids were in the witness-protection program."

Promising himself he wouldn't rise to the old man's bait, Gabriel put his hand first on one twin's head and then the other's. "This is Justin and this is Jared."

"'Bout time I met you two. Kinda small for five-year-olds, aren't they?"

"Walter…" His father's name came out in a low, warning growl.

"You always were touchy." Walter turned to squat before the boys. "You know how to shake hands like men?"

"Yessir," Justin said shyly, holding out his small right hand and nudging Jared to do the same. "Daddy taught us."

There had been precious few extras Gabriel could give his sons these past couple of years, so he'd concentrated on those small but important things he could provide. Like a firm handshake and the ability to look a person in the eye. Small fries to some folks, but if his boys were going to swim and not sink in Walter Brant's world, they'd need self-confidence.

One bushy eyebrow raised, Walter took each of the boys' hands in turn. "Well done," he said at last. Grudgingly. As if he'd expected to catch Gabriel in some parenting gaffe. "I guess you must be my grandsons, after all. But tell me, how am I gonna tell the two of you apart?" Walter squinted up at Gabriel. "You didn't tell me they were identical."

"That's because they're not, to me," Gabriel muttered between clenched teeth.

Walter ignored the admonition as he turned back to Justin and Jared. "Hungry?"

"Yessir."

"Then quit makin' my porch sag and come on in the house. I got SpaghettiOs and fruit cocktail." Holding open the front door, Walter challenged Gabriel with his glance. "And I just got a fresh loaf of Wonder Bread."

Gabriel didn't bite.

The house hadn't changed. The living room still had the same furniture his mother had picked out long ago. Sofa, end tables, TV, Walter's La-Z-Boy, Marjorie's reading chair, her upright piano—the lid closed over the keys—and a table with a huge lamp, standing in front of the picture window. The fancy lampshade was still wrapped in plastic. Walter hadn't even removed the knickknacks over the mantel. The small dining room behind the living room was as it had been when their original family of four sat around the old oak table each Sunday for Marjorie's pot roast dinner. Gabriel bet the room hadn't been used at all since his mother had died seven years ago.

Yet nothing looked neglected. Everything was in good repair, in the exact place it "should be," without a speck of dust in sight. The house at 793 Chestnut represented a solid, unchanging universe, controlled, as it always had been, by Walter.

Gabriel was having difficulty breathing.

Walter had set the kitchen table for four. "You

can wash up right here. I got this out of the attic for the boys."

Gabriel recognized the stool his father had made in his basement workshop. Gabriel and his older brother, Daniel, had used it to wash up at the kitchen sink for years, until Walter eventually had determined they were "man enough" to stand on their own two feet. That was the thing about Walter. He wasn't mean. He just insisted that life proceed according to his timetable. You could be a son of a bitch without being mean.

Gabriel helped his boys wash and dry their hands as Walter dished out four servings of SpaghettiOs. A small Pyrex bowl of fruit cocktail sat at each place, along with a glass tumbler, knife, spoon and paper napkin folded into a triangle. A milk carton, wrapped loaf of bread and tub of margarine were in the center of the table. Nothing more than was absolutely necessary.

"Need phone books?" Walter asked, as Justin and Jared climbed into their chairs.

"We can kneel, Grampa," Justin replied. Gabriel winced. Walter couldn't know just how much the twins had learned to make do since Katrina. With a nod from Gabriel, both boys began to eat with gusto.

"I called the school," Walter said, pouring milk into everybody's glasses. "They wouldn't let me register the boys—you have to do it. Tomorrow. They're expecting you."

"Can't it wait till after Thanksgiving?"

"These two need to be in school. The sooner, the better."

Gabriel knew that. He didn't need to be told. Didn't need to be sitting at his father's table, feeling a lot more like he was seventeen and lacking in judgment than thirty-four and a father himself. Maybe he should have taken one of those positions he'd considered in Atlanta or New York City. Problem was the only housing he would have been able to afford in either place wasn't fit for the cockroaches, let alone his sons.

"You talked to Daniel recently?" Walter asked, changing the subject, as if he'd settled the whole school issue.

"No." Gabriel replied cautiously to this loaded question. "How's he doing?"

"Coming up on his twenty years." His older brother was career army. "But I don't see him retiring. Dangerous as his job can be, he loves it. Plus, we need men like him."

Jab.

Gabriel had done his own time in the service. The Coast Guard, on Lake Erie, much to Walter's dismay. An even bigger disappointment was that Gabriel had been assigned to the mess and had discovered he loved cooking, even under military circumstances. After his discharge, he'd entered culinary school. Women's work and a waste, in Walter's mind.

"Daniel going to be stateside for the holidays?" Gabriel asked, as if the jab hadn't found its mark. "The more people around, the more I like cooking."

"What makes you think you're cooking?"

"It's the least I can do, if you're putting a roof over our heads." Temporarily. Only temporarily, until the job he was set to start on Monday earned him enough for the deposit on an apartment. Temporarily, while he built up his savings again and looked around for the right town, the right city to start his own restaurant. Again. "I'll shop tomorrow for Thanksgiving dinner. After I register the twins."

"It's not going to be highfalutin French stuff, is it? Or worse yet, Cajun. That spicy junk gives me heartburn. I like my Thanksgiving dinner traditional."

"Turkey. Chestnut stuffing. Cranberry sauce. Mashed potatoes. Gravy. Green beans. Pumpkin pie. Traditional enough for you?"

Walter looked suspicious. "If you make real whipped cream for the pumpkin pie, I guess. Daniel won't be home, though."

"You have any friends or neighbors you want to invite?" Now there was a rhetorical question. Walter, a retired union steward, had always been a curmudgeon, set in his ways and absolutely sure of his opinions. Marjorie had made and kept friends—never any she brought home—but Gabriel would be surprised if his father was still on speaking terms with his drinking buddies down at the VFW.

Walter didn't answer as he got up and headed for the stove. "You boys want seconds?"

"I do," said Justin. "You're a good cook, Grampa."

The look Walter shot Gabriel was one of pure triumph.

MINUTES AFTER THE LAST of her students had been dismissed, Olivia Marshall surveyed the disaster that was her kindergarten classroom. Hastily, she put away costumes that had spilled out of the dress-up box. Construction paper scraps littered the floor beneath the low tables. And the wastebasket beside the paint-smeared sink overflowed with used paper towels. She absolutely could not, *would not* leave this mess for the custodial staff.

"Ms. Marshall!" Five-year-old Eric Sedley, on the verge of tears, dashed back into the room. "I forgot my turkey! I can't go home without my turkey!"

Stepping quickly to his desk, Olivia retrieved the pinecone-and-pipe-cleaner bird, covered with glitter, that had been the last project of the short-ened day. "Now scoot, before you miss your bus!"

"The driver said she'd wait for me." Eric clutched his handiwork to his chest. Tears averted, smile in place, he ran from the room. "Happy Thanksgiving, Ms. Marshall!" echoed in the corridor.

It would be pointless to remind him to walk.

Early dismissal before a major holiday guaranteed pandemonium. Because—unlike most of the faculty—Olivia didn't have to rush home to get ready for tomorrow's feast, she'd spend the afternoon tidying her classroom.

"Ms. Marshall." The voice of Kelly Corona, the school clerk, crackled over the intercom. "I'm sending a Mr. Brant your way. I've just enrolled his twins, and they'd like to meet you and see their classroom before Monday."

Great. She surveyed her image in the stainless-steel towel dispenser mounted over the sink. If the disorder in the classroom didn't scare them off, her appearance might.

Pulling the elastic band from her hair, she quickly retamed her ponytail. Mr. Brant? The only Mr. Brant living in Hennings was Walter… Unless… With a quickening heartbeat, she shrugged out of the paste-covered smock she had on, shook glitter from her trousers and smoothed her top. Although there was nothing she could do about the smiley face "tattoo" Fiona Dunne had drawn with marker on the back of her wrist, she managed a quick hand wash and cursory cleaning of her fingernails, which always seemed to have crayon embedded under them. Before she could dry her hands, her three visitors were standing in the doorway.

Olivia couldn't determine who looked more uncomfortable—the boys or the man who stood protectively beside them. She might have passed him on the street without recognizing him, but face-to-face, how could she ever fail to remember those

piercing blue eyes? They could only belong to
Gabriel. A good six inches taller than she was and
solidly built, the adult version of her childhood
friend would have struck her as more than handsome if his features hadn't been shadowed by a
scowl that seemed indelibly etched.

"Come in." She hastily dried her hands. "Please,
don't be put off by the mess. I assure you it's
creative chaos. I'm Olivia Marshall."

He held out his hand. "Gabriel Brant," he said,
as if she were a complete stranger. Her own moment
of recognition was muddled by his faint Southern in-
flection. The Gabriel Brant she'd known years ago
had been a scrappy blue-collar Hennings through
and through. "These are my boys, Justin and Jared."

Oh, my. Identical twins. Same ill-trimmed mops
of tawny hair. Same intense blue eyes. Same wary
stance. She'd have her work cut out for her, keeping
them straight. At least they weren't dressed the
same. In fact, their outfits looked as if they'd been
chosen haphazardly from some yard sale.

She knelt before the boys. "So who's Justin and
who's Jared?"

One of the twins raised his hand. "I'm Justin.
He's Jared."

"Well, I'm Ms. Marshall, and I'm going to be
your teacher."

The boys didn't seem to know what to think.

"Would you like to play with our BRIO town,
while I talk with your dad?"

"What's a BRIO town?" Justin asked.

She led the boys to a carpeted corner where interlocking BRIO train tracks surrounded a town that changed every day, depending on her students' imagination. Because of the Thanksgiving skit and the turkey craft project, the miniature village had been neglected today. It was probably the only spot in the classroom that didn't look as if a tornado had struck it.

"There are DUPLOs, too," she said, pointing to a crate filled with blocks in primary colors. "If you want to make your own buildings."

Although their eyes sparked with longing, the twins turned to their father nervously.

"It's okay," he said. "Ms. Marshall said so."

Justin and Jared settled down to play, but with a hesitation that puzzled her.

When she turned back to talk to Gabriel, he seemed hesitant, as well. As if judging how much he should disclose. "Where we've been living," he said at last, "there weren't many resources. And if someone managed to get a little extra, he guarded it fiercely. The boys have learned to make sure they're reading the signs right. If it's okay for them to touch something that doesn't belong to them."

She tried to take in his statement without making judgments. After ten years as a teacher, she knew not to pry. Besides, underlying family issues always came to light in their own time. But where had this family lived, that sharing was so difficult?

"You did say Gabriel Brant?" she asked instead, proceeding cautiously. "Daniel's brother? Walter's son?"

"Guilty as charged."

"Do you remember me? One summer when you were ten and I was eight, you actually let me tag along after you. I think all your other friends had gone off to various day camps that year."

His chuckle wasn't much more than a grunt. "I do remember. But what happened to the pigtails and glasses?"

"The pigtails have been known to appear now and then, usually on field days, but laser surgery finally did away with the need for glasses."

He studied her carefully. "Your aunt's a great lady," he said. "How is she?"

"Aunt Lydia died six years ago." Olivia waved her hand to ward off any sympathy. "She was seventy-eight. Right up until the end, she said she'd had a wonderful life." The best part, she'd claimed, was having the opportunity to raise her grandniece.

"I still live in the house," Olivia continued. "At the end of every year, I give a party for my students and their parents. On the veranda. I serve refreshments using Aunt Lydia's recipes. Although I'm not the cook she was, I can follow directions." She grinned. "Sort of."

Gabriel glanced at his boys as they played in the corner, one providing quiet commentary and the other eerily silent. "Sounds like a good time," he said without much conviction. "If we're still here."

"This isn't a permanent move to Hennings?"

"That depends on whether I find a better job than the one I have lined up here."

Olivia decided to let that explanation suffice. "Tell me a little about the boys. About the school and the program they're transferring from."

His expression darkened. "This is the first opportunity I've had to enroll them anywhere."

"Did they go to preschool?"

"No. But I read to them. We count together. When I cook, they help me measure. They're bright," he said. His pride had an edge. "They'll catch up."

"Of course. Anyway, this is kindergarten," she assured him, trying to ease his defensiveness. "We don't start drilling for college entrance exams until first grade."

When he didn't respond, she prodded him. "That's teacher humor."

Preoccupied with watching his sons, he largely ignored what she was saying. He seemed to have fewer social skills now than he had as a ten-year-old.

"What's this?" The boy Olivia thought might be Justin broke the uncomfortable silence. He stood at her desk, pointing to the pinecone turkey she'd made.

"Why, that's a Thanksgiving turkey. Would you each like to make one to go on your dinner table tomorrow?"

"Yes, ma'am."

"We have to get going," Gabriel said, his brusque manner reminding Olivia of his father.

"Please, stay a few minutes more," she urged, bringing her thoughts back to her responsibility. Her new students. "This is such a simple project. And if the boys have fun today, they'll look forward to returning on Monday."

Instantly, she knew she'd hit upon Gabriel's soft spot. What was best for his sons. Before he could change his mind about staying, she cleared room at the craft table, dusted glitter off four chairs, then laid out fresh materials.

"Sit, Daddy," Justin urged, plopping down in a pint-size chair as Jared wordlessly claimed the seat next to him. "You can help."

Next came a scene Olivia never tired of watching. When a new parent first sank onto a kindergarten chair. Would the adult handle it with nonchalance, with self-deprecating humor, or with a sense that this was a deliberate assault on his ego? Over the years, Olivia had come to view it as a remarkably accurate test of character.

Gabriel Brant sat warily. As he'd sat many years ago on her aunt's antique wicker porch furniture. Aunt Lydia had served them homemade lemonade and gingersnaps. The memory tugged at Olivia now. She remembered how, at the end of the summer, Aunt Lydia had said, "He's a fine boy with a good imagination. Let's hope Walter Brant doesn't drum the imaginative part clear out of him."

As Olivia showed the twins how to twist brown pipe cleaners to form the turkey's head, legs and feet, and then demonstrated how to secure them in the pinecone's "tail feathers," Gabriel helped. Remarkably, his large hands were adept at this, his patience—with the boys—infinite. He never seemed to become more comfortable, though, only more determined. To accomplish this small task for his sons. Only when they'd finished shaking glitter onto the cones, and both Justin and Jared, who'd looked so sober upon entering her classroom, were smiling shyly, did Gabriel appear to relax.

She handed him the second demonstration bird she'd made today. "Now you can each have a turkey at your place tomorrow."

"What about Grampa?" Justin asked. "He'll need one. We're staying with him. Every day we're gonna walk from his house to school."

Interesting. When Gabriel had left town after high-school graduation, Olivia had heard rumors that it was because Walter and he were such polar opposites they couldn't stand to be in the same room. What had happened to bring Gabriel back?

He offered no explanation.

"I'll give you another one I made earlier with the class," she said, rising. "That way no one gets left out." Returning to the table, she handed a fourth turkey to Gabriel and then spoke to the boys. "So do you think you're going to like coming to school?"

"Yes, ma'am," Justin replied, but Jared only stared at his turkey.

"Jared," Gabriel said gently. "Look at Ms. Marshall when she's talking to you."

Jared did. Self-consciously. There was intelligence in his eyes, but deep uncertainty, as well. Although he made the requisite eye contact, he didn't speak.

"Well, I'm looking forward to having you both in my class. Let me get your dad a list of the supplies you'll need."

As if glad to be dismissed, Gabriel rose. When she handed him the list of pencils, crayons, glue sticks, tissues, change of clothes and more that was the standard request of kindergarten parents, he blanched. "They'll each need all these?"

"Yes," she replied. This was always the ticklish part. "But if, for any reason, you can't provide the supplies, I do have a discretionary fund…."

"I'll see they have what they need by Monday." His expression hard, he looked her in the eye. "Don't do me any favors. Don't offer any charity."

She was stung by the vehemence of his words.

As he turned to leave, it was as if he'd thrown a switch, shutting her out completely. In retreat, the set of his broad shoulders was stiff. The light touch of his hands on his sons' heads was gentle, but nothing else about Gabriel Brant was soft or yielding. Nothing that indicated the return to Hennings was the least bit pleasant for him.

What had life dealt her childhood friend to harden him so?

CHAPTER TWO

AFTER GABRIEL LEFT with his boys, Olivia didn't have time to puzzle over his prickly behavior before Kelly poked her head around the door frame.

"So did you like the early Christmas present I sent you?" the perpetually cheery clerk asked.

"I haven't had a minute to eat it," she replied, indicating the cupcake Kelly had sent to the classroom earlier. Olivia deliberately misunderstood the question.

"Not that, silly! Gabriel Brant." The clerk entered the room with a mischievous grin. "He didn't want the twins split up. I could have put them in Megan's class. She has the same number of students as you. But she's married."

Matchmakers. Hennings was full of them. "Are you forgetting the odds are fairly high Mr. Brant is married, too?"

"Oh, no," Kelly countered. "On the registration form he left the space for the twins' mother blank. I'm assuming he's unattached."

"That's a pretty dangerous assumption."

It wasn't that Olivia wasn't looking for love. Her aunt Lydia, the town librarian for many years, had raised her on a diet of fairy tales and adventure stories. Princesses in towers and princes on stallions. And happily ever after. They were the same tales she shared with her kindergarteners. Only now she occasionally changed the endings to have the princess do the saving.

"And you seem to forget," she added, "he's the parent of my two newest students. There must be a clause in my contract prohibiting a teacher from entering into a relationship with a parent."

"No. You can't date an administrator. And you can't engage in public lewdness. Otherwise, what you do in private is pretty much your own business."

Olivia slipped her arm around Kelly's shoulders. "I'll cut you some slack because this is your first year in the system. But FYI, the written rules and the unwritten rules can be poles apart." She didn't want to sound like a prude, but ten years' experience had taught her that teachers were still considered the most public of public servants. And single teachers? Their extracurricular activities were always scrutinized. "Besides, you're kind of jumping the gun, aren't you? Married or not, the guy just walked through the door."

Kelly shrugged. "The early bird, and all that. Hey, maybe he's separated. Maybe he needs a soft shoulder to lean on."

"You're incorrigible."

None of Kelly's musings answered the question of Gabriel Brant's marital status. He did have two sons. At some point there must have been, or else there still was, a significant other in the picture. Quite frankly, Aunt Lydia's lovely fairy-tale fantasies—and fantasies they were—made it hard to settle for anything less than magic. Olivia did know one thing with certainty, however. There was no fairy dust on affairs with married men.

"Well, what are you going to do?" Kelly pressed.

"What I'm going to do," she replied, "is catch a late lunch, then come back and straighten up this classroom. Want to join me for a bowl of chili at the diner?"

"I'd love to, but Don's parents are driving in tonight. If I don't get home and run a vacuum cleaner and a dust cloth around the house before then, his mother will drop not-so-subtle hints all weekend about my housekeeping skills. As if her only child and heir apparent shouldn't share the responsibility."

"As if you had nothing better to do with your time. Just how many are you having for dinner tomorrow?"

"Eleven. So one more wouldn't cause any more stress. You know you can change your mind and join us."

"Thanks." Olivia was tempted. "But the Meals on Wheels volunteers count on us holiday subs." And the elderly they served counted on a smiling face and a little company on a day when they knew others would be inundated with friends and family.

Olivia understood the feeling. "And the diner's doing the turkey dinners this year. At the end of my shift, I get take-home. Marmaduke will see that I don't go hungry."

"If you say so. But you can always stop by for dessert."

"I might do that. Just to run a white glove over your dusted surfaces."

"Don't encourage my mother-in-law."

When Kelly left, Olivia put on her coat, scarf and gloves. She couldn't find her hat, and she wondered whether one of her students had worn it home. Finally giving up the search, she headed for the diner, not a block from the school. The biting air made her wrap her scarf more tightly around her neck. Although the temperatures had been right for the season, there was still no sign of snow. A big disappointment, in Olivia's mind. What were the holidays without snow? The skeletal tree limbs arching overhead appeared downright spooky, as if Halloween still lurked. The branches needed at least a light dusting to flip the calendar to the appropriate page. *This is the famous New York snow belt,* she silently reminded the leaden sky. *So produce!*

She pushed through the diner's doorway into the crowded and steamy interior. "Olivia!" several people called out as she made her way to an empty stool at the counter. Ignatz, the ancient cook, winked at her from his side of the pass-through.

"The usual?" Maggie, one of two midday waitresses, asked from behind the counter, her Christmas bell earrings tinkling cheerily.

"Yes, please." Although, suddenly, Olivia wanted something unusual. It was such a strange and overwhelming sensation. A craving. An itch. A nameless longing. For something she'd never experienced before. She couldn't even tell if what she wanted was food or something bigger. Some adventure right out of a genie's lamp.

But what she got was chili and a large glass of milk.

"Thanks, Maggie." The odd feeling lingered as familiar voices around Olivia hummed in conversation.

"Who knows what your usual will taste like come Monday," Maggie said. "Ignatz's last shift is Saturday."

"That reminds me, I have a little retirement present for him. I'll bring it by Saturday afternoon. So who's the new cook?"

"Marmaduke's talking to him now." Maggie nodded to a booth in the corner. "I know the boss is relieved to finally sit down with him face-to-face. He got so many responses to that Internet ad, but he hired this guy on his reputation and his connection to Hennings."

"His connection to Hennings?" It couldn't be.

"By way of New Orleans. He's definitely easy on the eyes, but it's anyone's guess what the specials are going to taste like. Spi*cy,* I'm betting."

Olivia turned to see the owner of the diner in conversation with a man who had to be Gabriel Brant. His back was turned to her, but she could see the crowns of two small heads beside him. Justin and Jared. Someone had put crayons on the table. She could see a small hand coloring a place mat.

So this was the job Gabriel had taken until something better came up elsewhere. From the short interview they'd had in her classroom, she suspected he wasn't thrilled about the opportunity. Why not? Marmaduke, who'd started out as a short-order cook himself and still worked the breakfast shift, was known to be an excellent employer. One who hadn't forgotten his roots. One who prided himself on providing his employees with jobs that could actually pay the bills.

At that moment, Sasha, the second waitress, brought a tray to Gabriel's table and began to clear dishes. Stretching out his arm, Marmaduke rose to leave. The two men shook hands. The twin on the outside of the bench seat turned around and spotted Olivia. His tentative wave melted her heart.

She ate her chili and drank her milk and wondered—for the umpteenth time—if she would ever have children of her own. After getting her degree, she'd turned down a more lucrative teaching position in a bigger system to come home and help her aunt as that extraordinary woman's health began to fail. It was the least Olivia could do, after all her aunt had done for her.

Plus, she loved Hennings. Loved the big, old Victorian house in which she'd grown up, loved the small city's quirky rhythms, loved knowing her contributions made a difference. Her students became her children for ten months, and although she enjoyed watching them grow beyond kinder-garten, she always felt a sadness at the end of the school year, when she could no longer pretend they were hers.

Someone tugged at her shirttail. "Teacher?"

She looked down to see Justin and Jared stand-ing next to her stool, colored place mats in hand. Their father, serious and eagle-eyed, watched from the booth.

"Hello," she said. "I can see you've both been busy."

"We want to give you our pictures," Justin said. Olivia had determined that Justin was the twin who did all the talking. "Mine's a dog. If I could have a dog, I'd want him to look just like this."

Olivia took the picture and examined it. Two primitive figures cavorted across the drawing space. One, an obviously happy child, the other, an enor-mous dog. "This is very good, Justin. Do you know the story of Clifford, the big red dog?"

"The bookmobile lady read it to us."

"Well, we have that book in our classroom. On Monday, when you come to school, I'll find it for you. In fact, we'll read it together."

As Justin's eyes grew wide with anticipation,

Olivia felt a fairy godmother pleasure at being able to grant this simple favor.

"So, Jared," she said, turning to the quiet twin, "let's look at your picture."

Silently, he handed it to her. In the corner, three sad circle faces peered out of a tiny car. A swirl of brown and black and blue covered the rest of the paper, threatening to engulf the travelers. Stick figures floated in the deluge.

"Tell me about your drawing, Jared," she said ever so softly.

"It's what he experienced during Katrina," a deep voice replied, equally softly. Gabriel stood over his sons. "It's all he draws, in one variation or another. I figure if I let him get it out on paper, the nightmares will eventually stop."

And he'll eventually talk again, Olivia thought. She'd watched CNN, horrified as the hurricane had devastated a city. But that was two years ago. Evidently, to this little boy, the horror still hadn't diminished.

"Maybe I'm wrong, though," Gabriel said. "It hasn't happened yet."

"I don't think you're wrong," she replied, looking into adult eyes that held a world of pain. "Now that the boys will have the structure of home and school, I think you'll see a marked improvement."

The set of his jaw told her he wasn't convinced, and made her wish she could offer him a guarantee.

She turned to the boys. "Thank you for my

pictures. Would you like me to hang them in the classroom or on the refrigerator in my house?"

"In your house," Justin said. "So you won't forget us."

"It's not likely I'll ever forget you two," she replied, placing a hand on each twin's shoulder. Every kindergartener who walked through her classroom doorway needed her, but clearly these two were special. Their needs ran deep, maybe deeper than a single teacher could or should explore. Would she be able to help? She looked into the wary eyes of their father. Would he let her?

Suddenly, for Gabriel, the air in the diner was too close. He nudged the boys toward the cash register, but they wanted to linger with Olivia. She'd won them over already, which was a good sign they'd settle into school. If the memory of his own schoolboy crush on one pretty second-grade teacher rang true, his sons would be head over heels in love with doe-eyed Ms. Marshall before next week was out.

He wasn't certain he wanted the boys to form that great an attachment to anyone or anything in Hennings. The diner job was fine for starters. Knowing the difficulty of getting and retaining good cooks, Marmaduke paid well. Wanting to distance himself from fast-food places, he served traditional comfort food, but he was open to new ideas. Experimentation. Although he wouldn't change his long-established menu, he'd promised Gabriel the daily specials would be his to play with.

Even so, Gabriel planned on using his off time to use the public library's Internet hookup to find a better position. Most likely an out-of-town position. And that would mean a commute. Or a move.

As he stood in line to pay for his lunch, he watched his boys with Olivia. Somehow, he didn't think she'd approve of him uprooting the twins again. She seemed like the quintessential kindergarten teacher—sweet, traditional and rooted. But he firmly believed he and his sons could make it anywhere—hadn't they already?—as long as they were together.

When his turn at the cash register arrived, Marmaduke refused to let him pay. Gabriel fought the urge to insist, but his new boss matter-of-factly told him all employees got one full meal per shift. He should consider today a signing bonus. Finding it almost impossible to regard the act as a handout, Gabriel switched his attention to Jared and Justin. "Ready to shop for turkey day?"

"Grampa says we need more PasgettiOs," Justin said, waving goodbye to Olivia.

"Oh, I think my leftovers will replace the Grampa Walter special for a few days. Then we'll think about buying more O's."

"I like SpaghettiOs," Olivia said from her stool as Gabriel opened the diner door.

"Heaven help us," he muttered, stepping out into the cold.

"When are we gonna see snow?" Justin asked,

trudging alongside his father as the three made their way the few blocks back to Walter's house and their car.

"Any day now. And if it snows enough, I'll take you sledding on Packard Hill."

The boys, who'd spent their short lives in a climate that didn't require winter gear of any sort, gave him puzzled looks.

"Trust me," Gabriel said, opening their car door so the boys could pile in, "you're going to love it." Hey, that was the first positive thing he'd said about the return to Hennings. Maybe Ms. Olivia Marshall's quiet optimism was contagious.

At Wegmans, they made an "I spy" game out of shopping for their Thanksgiving groceries. The boys were wide eyed at the hustle and bustle, the colors, the choices, the piped-in music and the employees stationed throughout the store, handing out food samples.

For his part, Gabriel was glad to finally feel anonymous. Sure, he was a hometown boy, and a couple of people recognized him. But as far as being a Katrina evacuee, he didn't register on anyone's radar.

When the national media and the public at large had reached saturation point with the devastation and the hard-luck images, they'd moved on to the next breaking story, and Katrina—the good, the bad and the ugly—became a continuing reality only for New Orleans and the cities that had taken in the majority of those who'd had to flee. The lack of interest elsewhere was a curse, but at this particular moment in Hennings, it was also a strange blessing.

Back at 793 Chestnut, Walter met them at the door. "I got a surprise for you boys." The old man looked like the proverbial cat with a canary in its craw.

Gabriel suddenly felt uneasy, but as Justin and Jared dashed up the porch steps, he began to unload the bags of groceries from the car. By the time he made it through the front door, the twins were on the living-room floor, playing with a fleet of Tonka trucks. Brand-new construction equipment. Shiny yellow dump trucks, bulldozers, cement mixers, cherry pickers, earthmovers. You name it, Walter had bought it.

"The set you and Daniel had," Walter explained, all puffed up and looking proud of himself, "was metal. Pretty dinged up and rusted. Tetanus shots in the making. These are the same brand, but they're plastic. They're safer, plus they'll last longer."

Gabriel knew he should be thankful Walter was warming to this new role of grandfather, but... "Would you get the rest of the bags from the car?" he said. "I have stuff here that needs to go in the freezer."

Walter narrowed his eyes, paused a fraction of a second and then headed outside.

When the two men came together in the kitchen, Gabriel had curbed his initial negative reaction. "It's great you wanted Justin and Jared to feel at home," he said, trying to choose his words carefully. "But let's not go overboard with the toys. The boys are going to get bombarded with advertising between now and Christmas, and they've had so little these past two years, I don't want them to have unrealistic expectations."

"Are you finished?"

"Yeah."

"I've been buying a truck here and there for the past four years. Ever since I knew I had grandsons. Four years I've been waiting to meet them. There might be eight trucks out there. One a piece, for each birthday I've missed. So don't give me any crap now about overloading them with gifts."

Gabriel had no answer for that. In a tense silence, the two put away the groceries.

"Did you register the boys at school?" Walter asked at last.

"I did."

"Who's their teacher?"

"Olivia Marshall."

"That's good. She was an orphan—she'll understand the boys."

Gabriel felt the anger rise, hot and wild. Trying to keep his words from reaching the twins, he felt his voice come out thin and strained, like steam under pressure. "What are you talking about? My boys are not orphans."

"Their mother abandoned them."

"She brought them to me. Their father."

Only four years ago Gabriel had found out he was a father. Morgana, a woman with whom he'd had a brief affair, had shown up in New Orleans out of the blue and deposited one-year-olds Justin and Jared on his doorstep.

She'd been an exotic dancer when he'd first known her. When she arrived in New Orleans, she was an exotic dancer with a drug problem. But at least she'd had her head on straight enough to realize she couldn't continue to take care of the twins. His sons, she'd claimed. She'd even put his name on the birth certificates. So he'd taken a paternity test, and the boys were clearly his. As soon as the test results were in, Morgana had disappeared.

"Let's get this straight," Gabriel growled. "I've done some things I'm not all that proud of. You can beat up on me, but you are not to judge Justin and Jared for anything their father's done. Understood?"

"I understand you've got a burr in your boxers. Always have. And I'll be damned if I know why. But where your sons—my grandsons—are concerned, I was just stating a fact. Those two youngsters have had hard times to last four lifetimes. But they're home now. Me, I'm just glad they'll have a teacher who'll show them some kindness. Don't read any more into what I said than that."

His speech ended, Walter stomped out of the kitchen. Gabriel could hear the La-Z-Boy creak as the television came on.

Maybe he did have a burr in his boxers. After seventeen years of being on his own, of supporting himself, of building a reputation as a chef, he didn't find it easy starting over. Or coming to his dad, hat in hand. Walter, who'd never believed Gabriel could make it in the restaurant business in the first place. Thank God his boys were too young to understand the comedown.

Maybe this whole direction he'd decided upon was wrong. Maybe Hennings wasn't the place to regroup.

"I need to get some air," he said to the living room at large. "Boys, do you want to go for a walk with me?"

"Jared and I want to stay with Grampa and play trucks," Justin answered. "It's nice and warm in here."

Walter didn't take his eyes from the TV screen.

Outside, Gabriel walked in no particular direction, the low gray clouds matching his mood. He soon found himself standing outside the boys' school. Lights were on in one of the classrooms, and he could see Olivia Marshall gathering up her belongings. Why was she still at school well after dismissal on the afternoon before Thanksgiving? Didn't she have a better place to be? In fact, why was she still in Hennings at all?

When he'd hung out with her as a kid that one summer, she'd seemed so adventurous. As if the town wasn't big enough for her imagination. His friends had felt sorry for him, when they'd heard how he'd spent his vacation. With a girl. Two years younger than him, no less. He'd never admitted it, but it was one of the best summers he could remember. Olivia was smart as a whip. Fearless, too. He'd kind of expected the daring Olivia he knew then to grow up to be more than a demure hometown kindergarten teacher.

"Did you forget something?" Her grown-up voice at his side startled him. Not as much, however, as the very real, very close, very pretty woman's face that replaced the freckle-nosed girl he recalled.

He looked at the school and saw her classroom was dark now. How long had he been standing here? "Actually, I was remembering something."

"Good, I hope."

He didn't answer. The past didn't matter. The present didn't mean much to him, either. He was working on the future.

"Out for a walk?" she asked. "Don't tell me you have cabin fever already. Winter hasn't even begun."

"Being closed inside against the cold is going to take some getting used to."

"Well, when you're outside, you're going to have to remember to keep moving. Walk me home—I'm only a couple blocks out of your way."

How could he say no? He fell into step beside her, the soles of his shoes making crunching noises on the frozen sidewalk. He found it hard not to glance at her. Not to notice that the tip of her nose was already turning red and that the wisps of condensation as she breathed made her lips look soft and muted, as if she were an actress in a film and the director had called for the gauze over the camera lens. As if the mood aimed for was romantic.

Get a grip, Gabriel, he told himself. *You've been too long without.*

"I only know New Orleans from books and travel shows," she continued, her voice dreamy. "But with the warm climate and all the verandas and balconies and sidewalk cafés, I imagine the inside and the outside just melt one into each other."

"They did. Before the storm. Now…there are pockets. But the ease is gone from the Big Easy."

"You don't want to talk about it."

"No."

"Okay. Change of subject." Was she always this amenable? This upbeat? Didn't it exhaust her? "Are you bringing the boys to the Turkey Trot on Friday?"

"Turkey Trot?"

"It's a 5K road race up Main Street to the park. Race is a bit of misnomer, although I think they still give out a prize for the first person to cross the finish line. The real fun comes with the informal parade that tags along after the racers. It's kind of evolved over the years. People dress up. There's a prize for best seasonal costume. Parents push strollers. Kids ride decorated bicycles. Carl Obermeyer always walks on stilts, and his wife juggles."

Olivia picked up a stick and ran it, as a kid might do, along a wrought-iron fence that fronted a neatly kept yard. "One year," she continued cheerily, "a group of men from the Shamrock Grill attempted a synchronized lawn-mower routine. Turkey Trot's always a little nutty, but it's a good way to meet your neighbors and walk off the previous day's food. At the park, the outdoor skating rink officially opens. The whole thing's a lot of fun. Your boys would love it."

He stared at her. Slightly out of breath, she actually seemed as excited as a child at the prospect of this civic goofiness. "I don't know."

"Got better things to do?" There was mischief in her eyes. And a challenge.

"Hey, we just got into town yesterday. We've barely settled in."

"And today here you are out and about, enjoying our frosty air." She put a hand on his arm to stop him. "I can see you're already looking for an excuse to get out of the house."

She had him there.

"Do you want to talk?"

"What's this we're doing?"

"I mean, about your homecoming."

"No." With Lydia Marshall's old home in sight, he picked up the pace.

"So what about the Turkey Trot?" Olivia asked. Gabriel remembered that as a girl she'd been tenacious.

"Five K, you say?" He tamped down his frustration. Aimed for a reasonable tone of voice. "The twins are little, and we don't have a wagon or bikes." He didn't want to sound surly, given her enthusiasm for the event, but he didn't feel ready to plunge into the fishbowl that was small-town life, either.

"I believe there's still a Radio Flyer wagon in my garage," she replied, as if she wasn't in the least deterred by his excuse. "I'll bring it with me the day after tomorrow, and you can pull the boys in it."

He'd learned to mistrust seemingly generous offers. "Thanks, but—"

"It's the same wagon we used when we tried for the speed record down Packard Hill."

"Good God." The memory jolted him. "I still have the scars on my knees and elbows." He remembered how frightened he'd been, not because of his own injuries, but at the possibility that she'd be as badly hurt.

"Luckily, I don't have any reminders of my concussion."

"And you want me to put my boys in that demon wagon?"

"The parade route's flat. I promise," she said, her eyes sparkling, as if she knew he was running out of excuses. "And I'll introduce the boys to any of their classmates we meet on the way. So Monday won't seem like a sea of strange faces." She smiled. A radiant smile. "In front of City Hall, Friday, at one?"

He didn't know what persuaded him. That smile,

or the persistent memory of her earlier fearlessness. Of her tenacity. Her aunt's generosity. His lost innocence and childish optimism.

"Sure," he said, before he could figure out what he actually might be getting himself into.

CHAPTER THREE

THE OLD RED RADIO FLYER at her side, Olivia stood
in front of City Hall amid a crush of Turkey Trot
racers performing their warm-up stretches, and
neighbors jovially complaining to one another
about how they'd overeaten the day before. She
wondered if Gabriel would show. Had her excitement at seeing him again—especially later, alone—
come across as unprofessional? Having had
forty-eight hours to question her motives in asking
him to join her, she almost hoped he'd decide
against it. But then the twins would miss out, and
she didn't want that.

So what did she want? She'd been so unaccountably antsy the past few days that she'd be hard-
pressed to give a reply.

"Olivia!" Lynn Waters, director of the community rec center, squeezed through the crowd, confi-
dently wearing a headdress of turkey feathers and
a necklace of miniature gourds. "When can we get
together to begin work on the pageant?"

"Anytime." The annual children's winterfest

pageant was one of Olivia's favorite volunteer activities. No matter how precisely she and Lynn planned or how many times they rehearsed the kids, their charges always did something so spontaneous, so kidlike, so delightful at the performance, that no year was ever the same as the year before. And every one was memorable.

"I'm thinking of using real animals this year," Lynn said. "Ty Mackey's offered any or all of his."

"Even the potbellied pig?" Olivia laughed. "Does nothing frighten you?"

"Not having enough singers frightens me. I've gone over the list of kids who've signed up already, and we're still short on boys."

Olivia spied Gabriel making his way through the crowd, with Justin and Jared clinging to his side. It surprised her just how pleased she was to see him. Them. "I know two more boys who might be persuaded to join us," she said, thinking the camaraderie of the pageant might be what the twins needed to help them fit in and feel at home. "But I'll have to get back to you on that."

"Shall we have a planning session Sunday afternoon?"

"That's fine with me."

"Hi," Gabriel said, stopping in front of them. The one syllable slid over her senses like the intro to a mournful blues ballad. His eyes said he didn't want to be here. "I thought we might be too late." Wishful thinking?

His sons pulled at his hands. Justin glanced sideways at Olivia through lashes as thick as his father's, but Jared simply stared at the ground.

"Did you have a nice Thanksgiving?" Olivia asked.

"We survived," he replied.

For a moment Lynn studied Gabriel with interest, then raised an eyebrow and shot Olivia a silent, *Well?*

"Where are my manners!" Olivia exclaimed. "Lynn Waters, this is Gabriel Brant. And Justin and Jared Brant. Gabriel recently moved back to Hennings. His boys are going to be in my class."

"You're lucky," Lynn said to the twins. "Ms. Marshall was my daughter's first teacher. And she's still her favorite."

"Is your daughter five?" Justin asked.

"My daughter's now fifteen and in high school." Lynn looked directly at Gabriel. "And she babysits, if you and your wife…"

"We're not babies," Justin said, standing tall. "And Grampa watches us when Daddy can't."

Olivia could see the wheels in her friend's head spinning. Taking in this all-male scenario. But before Lynn could get the 411 on Gabriel's marital status, Olivia frowned and cleared her throat in warning.

"Well, I'd better find my husband," Lynn said. "He and his buddies at the Shamrock are trying to revive the lawn-mower brigade. They've sworn off alcohol until after their performance, so we'll see if that improves their synchronicity. Nice to meet all of you." She dimpled innocently at Olivia. "The wagon's a nice touch. It makes you look so…approachable." As if the Radio Flyer was some clever trolling device. "Bye!"

"Is that your wagon?" Justin asked, sparing Olivia the need to look at Gabriel.

"It is. Your dad and I used it when we were a bit older than you and Jared. I brought it today so that you can ride in the parade."

"Parade? Like Mardi Gras?"

"Not quite," she replied, suppressing a chuckle at the thought of the forthright women of Hennings baring their breasts for beads in near-freezing Turkey Trot temperatures. "But hop in. If we're going to take part, the first thing we need to do is get ourselves over to the face-painting station."

"Cold, wet paint on my face sounds really inviting," Gabriel said, pulling the zipper of his windbreaker as far up as it would go.

"It's just a dab," Olivia said, laughing. "It's kind of like a badge of honor, showing how tough we Hennings folks are. I'm thinking I'd like a pumpkin vine on my forehead." She turned to the twins. "How about you?"

"Can I get Spider-Man?" Justin asked, clambering into the wagon first and then helping Jared, whose eyes, despite his silence, registered real interest.

"I don't know if they'll have superheroes," Olivia replied, "but we'll check." She handed the wagon handle to Gabriel, who'd been listening carefully through this exchange. "How about you? Are you up for a superhero? If I recall, your favorite when you were ten was the Hulk. You told me my personal fave, She-Ra, was a wimp."

He took control of the wagon, but didn't exactly appear comfortable. He looked as if he didn't want her as a tour guide, pointing out highlights of the past. What was she thinking? She was presuming upon a very slight acquaintance. Apparently, it hadn't meant much to him then, and now it didn't engender the same warmth and ease it did in her.

"Take the wagon," she said, trying to regain her composure. "Don't worry about getting it back to me today. I won't need it until spring, when I'll use it to carry my seedlings from the nursery." Oh, great. Now she was babbling. What had gotten into her? Besides three pairs of blue eyes that said they needed relief from their recent experiences, even if one pair—*his* eyes—said he didn't need it from her.

"Have fun!" she said, trying to sound positive, wondering why she was so disappointed he didn't want her company. "If I see any of the boys' classmates, I'll be sure to bring them over for introductions."

She turned to leave, but Justin stopped her. "Teacher! Are we going to get our faces painted?"

"Your dad will take you."

"But I wanna see your face painted like a pumpkin."

"Maybe Ms. Marshall has plans to meet other friends," Gabriel said.

"No," she replied, without thinking. "I mean… I'm flexible."

"Come with us," Justin urged. "Pretty please with gumbo on top."

Gabriel still looked uncomfortable, but he seemed to soften. "How can you refuse a 'please' with gumbo on top?"

"Sounds messy," she said. Almost as messy as stepping beyond the absolutely professional with the father of two of her students. "But yummy."

"Then lead the way."

She did, as the mayor, standing high on City Hall's steps, bullhorn in hand, exhorted those participating in the race to assume their positions at the starting line.

"When the race starts," she warned the boys, "there'll be a big bang. It always makes me jump. But it's just the starting gun, letting the racers know they can begin to run."

"Noise doesn't bother them," Gabriel said, his voice low but bitter. "They've gotten used to close quarters and too little peace and quiet over the past twenty-seven months."

Twenty-seven months. Not rounded down to two years. As if each month was etched painfully into his memory. Distinct. Unforgettable. Now, that just wasn't fair. Her heart went out in sympathy.

When they approached the face-painting station, Jessie Nix and Sheria Hobson—middle-schoolers now—came forward, paint palettes in hand. "Hey,

Ms. Marshall!" they chorused, as Sheria looked at Gabriel. "Is this your boyfriend?"

"Sheria!" Olivia felt her cheeks tingle.

"Oops! My bad!" The girl dimpled with mischief and then shot Jessie a knowing look, which Jessie returned.

The girls knelt by the boys in the wagon. "Twins! Cool!" said Jessie. "Are you gonna let us paint your faces?"

"Can you paint Spider-Man?" Justin asked.

"I think he'd take too long, and you'd miss the fun," Sheria replied. "But we can do Spidey's web. Okay?"

Both boys nodded vehemently, and the girls got to work.

"It's cold and it tickles!" Justin exclaimed.

"Want me to stop?" Jessie asked.

"Nope. Ms. Marshall said it'll make me tough."

Olivia glanced at Gabriel and found he was staring at her. His intense gaze caught her off balance, and so she was unprepared for the signal beginning the race.

Not far from them, the starter's gun cracked.

With an indecorous squeak, she jumped, stubbed her toe on the curb and fell against Gabriel's chest. He was rock solid and smelled just good enough that in an instant she stopped thinking of him as the father of two of her students, or even as a childhood friend, and instead thought of him as a man. Plain and simple.

Although he definitely wasn't plain, and the situation sure wasn't simple. On top of which, the crowd pressing closely around them made it impossible to extricate herself.

In Katrina's aftermath, Gabriel had thought he was immune to the unexpected, but surprise didn't describe how it felt to find Olivia Marshall up against him. With so many layers of cold-weather clothing separating them, you'd think he wouldn't be able to feel her heat. But he did. Or maybe it was his own.

For more than two years, he'd been so busy eking out an existence for the boys and himself that he'd had no time for women. No time to acknowledge that he sorely missed their company. No time, now, to separate, as you might under normal circumstances, the simply social or the mildly amusing from the purely physical. He'd been without for so long, his reaction automatically skipped to physical want.

Olivia felt damn good.

"I'm sorry," she said, sounding breathy and smelling of peppermint. She struggled to pull away, but the crowd pushed them closer.

He could kiss her, she was that close. And if this had been a New Orleans Mardi Gras, no one would even blink. But this was the Turkey Trot in Hennings. A different atmosphere altogether.

"Daddy! Look at us!"

As Gabriel turned to look at his sons, his mouth grazed Olivia's forehead and created a spark of static electricity. She gasped and managed to free herself from his embrace—because embracing her was what he found himself doing. What he found himself wanting to do, until he noticed the open-mouthed gazes of two adolescent girls, paint palettes and hand mirrors frozen in midair.

"Did you trip?" Justin asked Olivia, innocent curiosity lighting his face.

"Y-yes… I'm afraid I did."

The girls dissolved in not-so-innocent giggles.

"Because your shoe's untied!" Justin exclaimed as Jared pointed to Olivia's hiking boot, its lace dangling.

"That must be the reason," Olivia replied, red-cheeked.

Gabriel really couldn't have said why he bent to tie her shoe. Reflex, perhaps. Because in the past four years he'd tied so many, at the twins' insistence. Anyway, as he bent on one knee and she did the same, their heads met in a painful bump.

"Ow!" Justin shouted in empathy.

"I second that," Olivia said, rubbing her head.

"Do you two need ice?" one of the face-painting girls asked.

Gabriel rubbed the already rising lump on his forehead. "That would be a good idea."

"We'll get some," the second girl offered, and both headed for the concession stand.

"If this was a typical November," Olivia remarked, tying her boot, then rising, "we could stick our heads in a snowbank."

"They have banks for snow?" Justin asked.

Gabriel thought of the difficulty of explaining this concept to kids who'd been raised in a warm Southern climate. "I think this is something that gets explained in kindergarten."

Olivia gave him a "gee, thanks" look before turning to the boys. "When we get snow—which we should by Christmas—you'll see that the snow on the sides of the road gets pushed into big humps called banks."

"If there's money in them," Justin replied solemnly, "maybe Daddy can get some for us. We need money."

Gabriel felt a sudden rush of shame, not at his son's honesty but at the fact that Justin—five years old—knew they were strapped.

"Everybody needs money," Olivia said, as if the statement was no big deal. "But you can't get it out of snowbanks. They're not regular buildings." Gabriel liked how she looked at Jared, as well as Justin, when she spoke. Including him, although he let his brother do all the talking. "Maybe they're called banks because that's where the snow gets saved until spring comes."

"I don't know," Justin said, shaking his head. "I'm just gonna hafta see one of these things."

Olivia laughed, and the sound on the crisp, cold air was genuine and refreshing. "After the first snow, your dad is going to have to take you sledding on Packard Hill."

"That's what I told them," he said, suddenly imagining how she'd looked on the Radio Flyer. Her gap-toothed smile lighting the way. Pigtails flying.

"What if it doesn't snow?" Justin asked. "What are we gonna do then?"

"Well, not sledding," she replied, "but there are lots of other fun things to do here. In fact, I was just about to ask your dad if he'd let you be in one of them."

"One of what?"

"It's our community winterfest pageant," she said, massaging her head. Her forehead had to hurt as much as Gabriel's did, but it was apparent she was trying to minimize the pain in front of the boys so as not to worry them. "You get to dress up and sing and celebrate the first day of winter and our famous cold weather. This year, we're going to have animals, too."

"Elephants?"

"No elephants, but farm animals like—"

"We're not theatrical," Gabriel said. Brants never had been. Walter, maybe. But only for a home audience. "Thanks, anyway."

"I wouldn't consider Ty Mackey theatrical," she replied, with an edge of determination Gabriel found challenging, "but he's the one providing the animals. Just think about it."

"Omigosh, we had to chip this out of the concession-stand cooler!" One of the face-painting girls returned with two paper cups of ice. "It's so cold today nobody's ordering anything but cocoa and coffee, and the ice had turned to one big lump." She handed a paper cup each to Gabriel and Olivia. "Whoa, I'm just in time. You guys have matching goose eggs."

"Thanks for the first aid, Sheria," Olivia said, pressing her cup to the lump on her forehead.

"No problem." Sheria waved to Justin and Jared as she melted back into the crowd, which now swept along in the wake of the racers. "Have fun, little Spidey dudes. Hope you like the webs we painted."

"How do we look, Dad?" Justin asked, turning his cheek for inspection.

"Awesome."

Sitting in the wagon, the boys threw their shoulders back and their chests out in minimacho postures, clearly pumped by their new superhero markings.

"Are you going to be all right?" Gabriel asked, turning to Olivia. She'd been so plucky as a girl, but there was something unexpectedly fragile about her as a woman.

"Of course," she replied, as if she read his thoughts and still wanted to appear tough as nails. "You'd better get going. I hear the lawn mowers revving up. And I think Ty's brought his llamas. The boys won't want to miss them."

"Are you going home?"

"No."

"Then you're coming with us. So that we can

keep an eye on you. I feel partly responsible for that crack on your head."

"Believe me, I have no intention of passing out on the parade route."

"But what if I do?" he replied, trying for lightness. An unaccustomed tone for him. "Then who's going to pull the boys in the wagon?" He didn't know why he suddenly wanted her company, but he did. "Don't you feel partly responsible for the lump on my head?"

"Daddy!" Justin pointed to a man on stilts, dressed as Uncle Sam and walking through the crowd, tossing candies to the kids. "That man is almost as tall as a house."

Olivia reached up, and one-handed caught several candies, which she gave to the twins. "Okay, boys, your first field trip in Hennings. Let's go."

Gabriel suddenly wondered if Olivia's unflagging fortitude was an act. If so, why did she need to have one?

Olivia felt his scrutiny. Would it have been more prudent to go home? But now they were moving forward, and there were so many people that it didn't look as if she and Gabriel were together, as in "couple" together. They were just part of the crowd, walking off too much turkey. Although after that little misstep back at the face-painting station, she couldn't help wondering—for just an inappropriate second— what it might be like to be paired up with him.

They hadn't gone more than a block when both

Olivia and Gabriel ditched their ice cups in a trash container. It was easy to forget about a bump on the head when you were so busy watching happy five-year-olds reacting to the sights and sounds of a town gone silly. Sheria had even doubled back to hand them a couple of kazoos, which the twins quickly mastered.

"This was a good idea," Gabriel said. "It was getting a little tense at Walter's."

"And you don't want the boys to suffer."

"Actually, Justin and Jared get along fine with my father. I can't figure that out, but I'm thankful for small miracles. It's Walter and me. We're the ones sniffing round each other like mistrustful dogs. I don't want the boys picking up on that."

She was surprised at his admission. Unfortunately, even if he didn't know why, she knew the root of his and Walter's disconnect. But it wasn't her place to explain it. Besides, she didn't want to say anything now and have Gabriel close down again. "You might talk to Marmaduke," she replied instead. "In addition to the diner, he owns some rental properties in town. I'm sure he'd make you a fair deal."

Despite the fact she thought of what she'd said as a neutral statement, he seemed to withdraw.

"Daddy," Justin interjected. "Jared's thirsty. Me, too."

"The concession stand's up ahead," Olivia offered. "I'll treat."

Gabriel glowered at her. "Don't."

"I just…"

"I can buy my boys a couple of drinks." His voice was low. Almost a growl. A warning. Then, more calmly, he said to the boys, "Do you want something cold or hot?"

Olivia was struck by how Gabriel's frustration simmered so close to the surface. How he had to exercise control to interact civilly with anyone other than his sons. If he hadn't been the parent of two of her students, she might have called him on it.

"We want a hot drink," Justin said. "Our noses are cold."

They stood in front of the refreshment stand, where Greer Briscoe waited to take their order. Olivia could have wished for anyone else. Seventy-two-year-old Greer was kindhearted, but she often exercised her right to behave as a self-professed "magnificent crone." The advantage of old age, she always said, was that you could dispense with conversational filters. You were old, and you were supposed to tell it as you saw it.

"Your nose looks cold, too, Ms. Marshall," Gabriel said, before turning to Greer. "Four hot chocolates."

"Whipped cream or marshmallows?"

"Whipped cream," he replied, without consulting Olivia. "But before you top the two for the kids, can you add a little milk to cool the hot chocolate?"

"You got it."

When Greer slid the drinks for the boys across the counter to Gabriel, she looked at Olivia.

"Olivia, hello. I'll be with you in a minute," she said, as if the fourth drink wouldn't be for Olivia. As if, of course, Ms. Marshall would be unattached.

"I'm with them," she replied without thinking.

"Oh?" Greer glanced at Gabriel and the boys with interest. "Wait a minute. I thought you looked familiar. You're Walter Brant's son. The Hurricane Katrina refugee."

Olivia saw Gabriel flinch at the loaded word.

"I prefer to be called a survivor," he said, his jaw tight.

"Well, you're certainly in the right company," Greer declared, passing the other two hot chocolates their way. "Olivia has the softest heart in all of Hennings. Why, as a little girl, she brought home every stray cat and injured bird…"

Gabriel didn't wait to hear the rest. He picked up the handle of the wagon and stormed away up Main Street, leaving Greer still rambling on and Olivia smarting.

The day could not end this way.

She picked up the two abandoned drinks and hurried after him.

When she caught up, he didn't slow his pace.

"Hold on!" she implored. "The boys will spill their hot chocolate."

He stopped abruptly to face her. "I was wondering what your game was."

"What are you talking about?"

"I've met other women like you, who get their

kicks doling out pity. Taking on the downtrodden. Feeling so satisfied when you save one of the hopeless from the brink."

Both boys were staring at the adults, worried expressions making their young faces seem much older.

"That is not what's going on," she insisted with a significant nod toward his sons.

"No? The offer to fund the boys' school supplies, the loan of the wagon, the willingness to buy drinks…"

"Have you been gone from Hennings so long you've forgotten what being neighborly means? Gabriel, this is me. Olivia."

Something flickered in his eyes—a light that disappeared as soon as it appeared. "Let me make this perfectly clear," he said. "We're not refugees. We don't need your pity. And we don't want your charity. We'll borrow the wagon for today, but I'll return it tonight. If my kids need something, I'll provide it."

He pulled the boys away and left her standing with two cups of hot chocolate and a guilty feeling in the pit of her stomach.

CHAPTER FOUR

SUNDAY NIGHT Gabriel lay in bed in Walter's spare room and stared at the face-shaped stain on the ceiling, which was illuminated by the streetlight outside the window. Before his return to Hennings, he'd never slept in this room. It held no memories for him. It should mean no more to him than some anonymous motel room. Yet his mind wouldn't quiet, and sleep eluded him.

Tomorrow was the twins' first day of school. His first day of full-time work in what seemed like ages. A degree of stability after twenty-seven months without any. He should feel an easing of that chronic pain between his shoulder blades. But he didn't.

As he kept replaying the past week in his mind, he twisted and turned on the uneven mattress, trying to find a comfortable position. But thoughts of living indefinitely with his father, of taking a job that was beneath him, and of Olivia and her patronizing Marshall Plan—especially thoughts of Olivia—made him punch the pillow in frustration.

He'd been so angry over her thinly veiled charity he hadn't yet returned the Radio Flyer. He didn't want to see her again. He was even thinking of requesting a transfer for the boys. To the other kindergarten class.

Even more disturbing than his anger had been the attraction he'd felt.

A scream cut through the still house. That would be Jared.

Gabriel sprang from bed, tripped over his shoes, banged his shoulder against the door frame, swore, and then staggered down the hall toward what had once been his and Daniel's room. Only to find the light already on and Walter kneeling by the edge of Jared's bed.

"He had a nightmare, Grampa," Justin mumbled sleepily from the adjacent bed.

"I know, son," Walter replied, his back to Gabriel.

As his father drew Jared close, Gabriel remained in the shadows of the doorway, prepared to intervene if necessary. Walter had seldom dispensed anything other than cold comfort to his own sons.

"Are you awake now?" Walter asked, his voice gruff but at the same time gentle. "Is that nightmare gone?"

Jared snuffled.

"Do you know where you are?"

"At your house," Justin replied for his brother.

"Your house, too. So you know what that means.

Nothing bad is gonna happen to you here. Either one of you. I won't let it. So those old nightmares are just gonna hafta find somewhere else to hang out. You understand?"

"Yessir," Justin said, yawning, as Jared nodded, his eyelids already at half-mast.

"Now close your eyes. I'm gonna stay right here until I hear you snoring."

Justin giggled sleepily. "Grampa, we don't snore."

"You better not. 'Cause I need my beauty rest in the next room. And if you go back to sleep real quick, I'll let you have Cocoa Puffs for breakfast."

"Daddy doesn't like Cocoa Puffs."

"He won't be the one eating them."

Walter remained kneeling between the beds. Only when both twins were fast asleep again did he stand and turn. The look on his face said he didn't know Gabriel had been behind him. Didn't appreciate the audience. Wordlessly, his stiff demeanor back in place, he brushed by his own son, switched off the light and then made his way downstairs. Gabriel followed.

In the kitchen, Walter lit a burner, got out a saucepan, honey, lemon juice and whiskey. "You want a nightcap?"

"No, thanks." Gabriel needed a clear head tomorrow.

"Suit yourself." Walter added a splash of water to the saucepan, then proceeded to make himself a hot toddy. "How often does Jared get nightmares?" he asked. Belligerently. As if Gabriel might somehow be to blame.

"Once a week. Sometimes more." This was the first one since the return to Hennings.

Stirring the ingredients in the saucepan over the flame, Walter didn't reply.

"You don't have to get up with him. When it happens again, I'll take care of it."

Walter slit his eyes. "You said *when* it happens again. Don't you mean *if?*"

"After twenty-seven months, I'm just being realistic."

"The boys are home now. You might see a difference. Don't be so negative."

"I'm going to turn in," Gabriel said, giving up on the idea of a real conversation, and not wanting to discuss the differences returning to Walter's house might make. "I just wanted to say…thanks. For being there this time. For Jared."

"No big deal."

Why was it so hard to give anything—even a simple thank-you—to this hardened old man? No gift, no effort, no accomplishment ever found easy acceptance. Certainly not during Gabriel's boyhood. He stared at his father. A man he'd never understand.

"What?" Walter asked, looking up and glowering. "You think it's a big deal I comforted a scared kid? You think I'm not up to something that simple?

Or you think I don't understand nightmares? Let me tell you, this Vietnam vet has had to cope with a few of his own through the years, and I'm not gonna let my grandson suffer, if I can help it. It's what you do for your own. It ain't worth the Nobel Bleedin'-Heart Prize. It's no big deal. So stuff your thanks."

Gabriel stormed out of the kitchen. He couldn't figure out what ticked him off more—the disconnect between himself and his father all these years, or Walter's sudden unexpected proprietary air toward Justin and Jared. An attitude that seemed to suggest Walter knew what was right for the boys while Gabriel didn't. Same old same old. Gabriel tried to calculate how many paychecks he would need before he could put aside enough for a deposit on an apartment.

He couldn't, wouldn't stay under his father's roof a minute longer than he had to.

ALERT TO THE ever-changing dynamics of five-year-olds, Olivia circulated on the playground. There were ten minutes to go until dismissal, and this Monday had been particularly difficult. Not only were her kids sky-high after the Thanksgiving break, but they were already gearing up for Christmas. Added to this usual excitement was the novelty of two new classmates, the jockeying for friendships, the testing, the rearranging of the pecking order. It didn't help that Jared hadn't spoken a word the entire day. Differences were not something kindergarteners automatically accepted. It was her job to see that the other children minded their p's and q's until he began to talk.

More than this, she felt deeply that it was her job to help him come out of his silent world.

What had looked, at first, like a game of tag in the far corner of the playground had developed into a scuffle. Olivia ran to intervene, and found Justin and Jared on the ground, wrestling with Milo Rollins. Two against one, the twins were getting the better of Milo. With difficulty—all three boys were exceptionally strong—she managed to separate them, as the rest of the class gathered in small knots to await the consequences they knew would come.

She took Milo firmly in hand on one side of her and Justin on the other. "Hold on to your brother," she told Jared. Silently, he did. Only a little out of breath, she instructed her students to line up. While the parent volunteer who was there to help the children get ready for dismissal watched the others, Olivia would deal with the combatants privately. She didn't have much time. Milo needed to be on the after-school day care bus as soon as the bell rang, and Gabriel presumably would be by to walk the twins home shortly thereafter. She needed to get to the bottom of the altercation with the children before she involved their parents.

Easier said than done.

Questioned in the corridor just outside the classroom, Justin and Jared presented a silent united front, and Milo seemed to take his cue from them. In fact, he seemed relieved the twins weren't talking, making Olivia think he'd been the instigator.

"I'm going to have to speak to your parents," she said at last. Still no reaction. "Do you understand fighting in school is not allowed?"

"Yes, ma'am," Justin replied, as Jared and Milo nodded. All three avoided making eye contact. With her and with each other.

"Then shake hands."

Reluctantly, they did.

"Now gather your things for dismissal." She propelled them toward the cloakroom, where the volunteer had the rest of the children ready and in three lines, for walkers, bus riders and after-school care.

Belle Polanski reached out and tugged on Olivia's slacks. "Ms. Marshall," she whispered. "Milo was teasing Jared 'cause he doesn't talk."

Olivia had thought as much, but she wanted to hear the truth from the boys themselves. She smiled down at Belle. "What have we decided about tattle-tales?"

Belle blushed, then made as if to lock her lips and throw away the key.

"Good girl."

Dismissal, as usual, was a blur. When it was over, Olivia was left outside under the school's portico with Justin and Jared.

"Does your dad know someone has to pick you

up?" she asked. "I can't allow you to walk home alone."

"Dad's working," Justin replied. "Grampa's gonna come get us. There he is!"

Sure enough, Walter Brant came limping along the sidewalk.

"Sorry," he said when he joined them. "Bum knee. Hates the cold. So, what did I miss?"

The boys had the good sense to look guilty.

"Something wrong?"

"I wanted to talk to the twins' father."

"He's working. I'm the grandfather. Shoot."

Conferences with anyone other than a child's legal guardian weren't the usual procedure, but the boys were living with Walter, after all. Olivia would stop at the diner to set up an appointment with Gabriel, but it couldn't hurt to lay the groundwork now. "The boys were involved in a playground fight—"

"All right!" Walter declared. The smile he shot his grandsons reflected real pride. "Show 'em right off the bat you're not sissies."

"Fighting is *not* tolerated," Olivia replied, fixing the older man with her best authoritative stare. "The boys understand that. The bigger issue is that, given the opportunity to explain the circumstances of the fight, they wouldn't."

"What about the other kids involved? What did they say?"

"The other child chose to remain silent, as well."

"Good. Nothing worse than a squealer."

She wasn't certain what prompted Walter's macho reaction, but she knew for certain she should have waited to discuss the issue with Gabriel. She didn't know what kind of environment the boys had come from in New Orleans. She didn't know what the dynamics were on Chestnut Street, either. But the classroom was her domain, and there peaceful coexistence and forthrightness ruled. She needed to make that clear.

"In kindergarten, we don't fight," she said, "and we own up to our mistakes."

"There's a big difference between kindergarten and the real world."

"Mr. Brant…" She began to launch into a rebuttal, then caught herself. "I'll make an appointment with Gabriel."

"Suit yourself." Unfazed, Walter looked at his grandsons. "We're gonna stop at the VFW on the way home, boys. I got some friends who wanna meet you. You ever play foosball?"

The twins seemed happy enough to leave with their grandfather, but Olivia wondered about their after-school activities under Walter's care.

As a sharp gust of wind slipped its icy fingers underneath her collar, she turned to reenter the building. She'd call Milo's mom—another single parent—at her work. Olivia had no doubt Regina Rollins would get to the bottom of the matter with her son. She and Olivia had three months' history together already. Good parent-teacher teamwork history. But Gabriel? His parenting skills and his motivations were unknown quantities. It wouldn't hurt to speak to him at the diner, face-to-face, if only to set up a time to speak on the phone later. Besides, she was curious to see what he'd done with Marmaduke's daily specials.

School business and culinary curiosity. Those were the only reasons she was making a personal visit to Gabriel Brant. Or so she tried to tell herself.

Then why was her heart beating just the tiniest bit faster as she pushed through the diner doorway later that afternoon? It had to be the slightly different coffee aroma wafting on the air. Or the prospect of *pain perdu,* which was listed as dessert on the specials board. Certainly not the stony-faced, broad-shouldered man in the red bandanna who'd taken Ignatz's place in the kitchen.

Although few of the tables were filled this late in the afternoon, Olivia took her usual stool at the counter.

"Merry Christmas, Olivia. I'll be with you in a sec."

Startled, Olivia swung around on her stool to see Maggie perched on a chair, hanging a garland over one of the big plateglass windows. Because she'd been focusing on Gabriel, Olivia hadn't noticed the waitress, who climbed down from the chair now to step behind the counter.

"Merry Christmas," Olivia replied. "Although I'd feel more in the holiday spirit if it would snow."

"You gotta make your own spirit," Maggie said, nodding toward a cheery crocheted snowman pin on the pocket of her uniform, just under a spotless handkerchief. "Regular or chicory?" she asked, holding up two coffee pots. "The chicory's new. Not sure it's going to catch on, mind you."

"What goes best with the *pain perdu?*"

"Beats me," Maggie replied. "Haven't tried it and can barely pronounce it. Although people who've dared to order it say it's good."

"Let's try the chicory. And the *pain perdu.*"

"An order of that fancy French toast!" Maggie called into the pass-through.

"How'd it go today?" Olivia asked.

"He can cook, that's for sure," Maggie replied, lowering her voice as she turned back to pour the coffee, "but he's a growly thing. Makes Marmaduke look like Mr. Cuddles."

"Do you think he'd have a minute free to talk to me?" When Maggie's eyebrows shot up in question, Olivia hastily added, "It's about the twins. School stuff."

"Sure." All the same, Maggie looked very uncertain. "Won't hurt to ask. You, that is. Me, if I'm not back in five, call the rescue squad. I'm the only waitress on duty till four-thirty." She disappeared into the kitchen.

Minutes later, the swinging door opened and Gabriel appeared, his usual scowl firmly in place. He set a plate in front of Olivia. On it were what appeared to be golden fried medallions of sliced baguette dusted with powdered sugar. It did look like French toast, but it smelled lusciously of orange. "Maggie said you wanted to see me."

Olivia really wanted to dig into the dessert, but professionalism prevailed. "I'd like to talk to you about Justin and Jared's first day of school. But if now's not a good time, let me know when I can give you a ring."

"Let's take care of it now," he replied without apparent enthusiasm. "Things are slow."

"Right up until fifteen minutes to dismissal, things went very well," she began. "Although Jared didn't speak."

"I didn't expect him to."

"As a teacher, I always set my expectations high," she replied gently, trying not to lose her composure under the relentless glare of Gabriel's blue eyes. She was accustomed to the rocky course of diplomacy when dealing with some parents, but she wondered why this one particular man seemed to knock her off balance. "It's surprising how often children rise to them."

That's the difference between hopelessly naive and realistic, Gabriel thought sourly. "I don't need a day-by-day report on Jared's behavior."

"I don't plan on giving you one." She sat up straighter. "I'm here because Justin and Jared were involved in a playground scuffle. I think the other boy involved teased Jared about not speaking, but none of the boys is talking. When I mentioned it to your father, he seemed to encourage the behavior. Both the fighting and the stonewalling."

"You discussed this with my father?" Gabriel tried to keep his anger in check. "Why the hell would you do that?"

"He seemed to sense something wasn't quite right when he picked them up. And he is their grandfather. You're all living under one roof."

"Don't remind me." He poured himself a cup of the chicory brew. Took a long swig, although it scalded the roof of his mouth. The pain somehow reined in his impulse to lash out at the woman sitting across from him. He had to get a grip on this feeling of his that everyone was the enemy. Or if not the enemy, then at least someone who was happy to throw a monkey wrench into the works. His works. "Look, I'd appreciate it if you'd discuss the boys only with me. My father's involvement stops at picking them up and watching them while I work."

"Okay. But about the fight—"

"I'll talk to the boys tonight." He turned to reenter the kitchen. "Eat your *pain perdu* before it gets cold."

On the other side of the door, he found himself staring into Maggie's wide eyes. "Table four needs busing," he said, as he went back to preparing individual ramekins of the chicken, beans and sausage cassoulet that would be the supper special.

Although Marmaduke had given him free reign in the kitchen, Gabriel still didn't like working for someone else. Not after years of being his own boss.

And he didn't like Olivia—or anyone else, for that matter—monitoring his boys' every move. Moreover, he was angry with himself for not having had the guts to return her Radio Flyer and be done with her.

He heard the kitchen door open, but he ignored it. If Maggie had another order, she'd shout it out.

Instead, Olivia came into view.

"Customers aren't allowed in the kitchen," he said, as he sautéed onions, garlic and parsley in bacon drippings.

"This was absolutely wonderful," she said, undeterred, holding out her empty plate and coffee mug. "And whatever you're making now smells heavenly."

He hoped she didn't intend to return for supper.

She placed the plate and mug in the sink. "Your boys are going to be okay. I can feel it."

He hadn't asked for her opinion.

"I'm still convinced it would help if they had an after-school activity." Lord, how she went on. "The added stimulation would be especially good for Jared. At some point he's going to want to express what he's taken in."

She was so full of theories. Meaningless, in the real world. Petty, in the face of the negative experiences Jared had suffered. Silently, Gabriel worked on, layering chicken, beans and sausage into the serving dishes.

"The more constructive interactions Justin and Jared have with their classmates outside school,"

she continued, "the more allies they'll have during
school. Familiarity breeds friendships."

"They have me. They have Walter."

"Yes. And the VFW. Their after-school field trip
today," she remarked sardonically.

Damn. Not quite Mr. Rogers's neighborhood.

Olivia took a step closer. As if merely entering
the kitchen wasn't a big enough invasion of his
space. "I know you turned me down once, but our
winterfest pageant is coming up and the kids always
have fun participating."

"Why are you so persistent?"

"I'm paid to persist. To do what's right for my
students." She arched one eyebrow. "Why are you
so rude?" She pointed in the direction of the dining
room. "I don't believe we'd finished our conversation before you stormed out."

"I'm paid to cook." He picked up a chicken leg
and shook it at her. "Poultry doesn't care if I'm rude.
Marmaduke didn't hire me because of my manners."

She looked as if she might laugh, but then quickly composed herself. "Tell me you know for certain
that Justin and Jared wouldn't enjoy taking part in
the pageant."

"All right. They can take part." He'd have said
anything to make her be quiet. Make her stop
staring at him. Make her leave.

"Terrific! The performance is on the twenty-
second of December at seven. There will be three
rehearsals. Saturdays at 10:00 a.m."

"That's not going to fly. I have to work Saturday mornings." That wasn't quite true. Marmaduke and he had sorted out a rotating work schedule, but the blanket statement should put an end to the pageant issue and still get Olivia to depart.

"If your father can drop them off, I'll bring them home."

Did the woman ever take no for an answer?

"If they don't have a good time," she added, an edge of challenge in her voice and a spark in her big brown eyes, "I won't pressure you to send them again."

She seemed pretty damn confident she could win his boys over in one morning. That in itself was enough for him to mark his territory. To say no. But what if the twins had a good time? What if they did make friends? What if Jared was stimulated enough to speak again? Could Gabriel deny them the opportunity?

"Okay," he agreed, torn between what was right for his boys and what he felt he could handle himself.

What felt right for him was minimal contact with this woman, who didn't seem to know how to stay out of his personal space. His business. Did she bully all her parents into doing what *she* thought was right for their kids? "I'll send them this Saturday, and then it's up to them."

Olivia seemed inordinately pleased as she left the kitchen.

And Gabriel knew that in a galaxy far, far away

he should feel pleased at the opportunity she was giving Justin and Jared. Should feel gratitude, even. But he couldn't shake the sensation that she'd taken his family on as a pet project.

And he didn't like it one bit.

CHAPTER FIVE

As with every Winterfest pageant in Hennings, chaos reigned at the first rehearsal. More children than expected had shown up, probably because a gloomy, unseasonal rain was falling outside and parents wanted a supervised place to park their kids for a couple hours that Saturday morning. Olivia and Lynn Waters were on the receiving end. Regina Rollins, who'd agreed to handle wardrobe, hadn't yet shown up. Approximately thirty kids ran around the rec center, which already sounded like a barnyard without Ty Mackey's animals. At least they were going to have enough singers.

"Henry Jacobson!" Olivia called to a former student of hers, now in fourth grade. "Stop twisting your sister's arm this minute."

"But she says I'm gonna hafta kiss Portia Kemp!"

"That's absolutely no reason to abuse Amanda," she replied, swiftly approaching the two to make certain Henry got her message.

As Olivia and Lynn had gone over the list of

kids who'd signed up early, they'd considered Henry for the role of Jack Frost and Portia for Mrs. Frost. Key roles. Apparently, word of their preliminary planning had leaked out.

"Besides," she added, putting her arms around each child, "I can assure you there's no kissing in this pageant."

Despite his earlier protest, Henry seemed just the slightest bit disappointed.

"Ms. Marshall!" Quentin Freeman approached her, holding out a CD. "I brought my favorite Christmas carol. You think we can use it this year?"

Olivia glanced down at "Grandma Got Run over by a Reindeer." "I think Ms. Waters has already chosen the music, Quentin, but I'll run this by her. Thanks for the input." Something glittered in her peripheral vision.

"Naomi! Put that down!" She abandoned Henry, Amanda and Quentin, to head off Naomi Tester, who'd looped a foil garland around her head like a crown. "Those are to go to the Methodist church for their fair. They're not for our pageant." Rescuing the garland and a large box of reserved Christmas decorations, Olivia slid them all on top of the cabinet that held bingo materials.

A series of loud chords, played in rolling succession, resonated from the piano in the corner. "Fannies on the floor!" Lynn called out from her bench at the keyboard.

No one sat.

Olivia began to circle the room in good border-collie style.

"You heard the lady!" a male voice bellowed. "Sit!" Walter Brant loomed in the doorway like a storm cloud, with Justin and Jared clinging to his sides. As the older man made his way through the room, the twins in tow, children began to sit down.

"Looks like you need a Marine sergeant to deal with these kids," he said, coming to a stop in front of Olivia. "I'll stay."

"There's no need," she replied, as Zach Edwards dashed by, pursued by Valencia Sanchez, with a rubber snake in hand. Olivia caught the snake's tail and Valencia bungeed back. "Oh, my!" Olivia said to the girl in mock surprise. "I thought you were in third grade, not kindergarten."

Valencia had the good sense to look apologetic.

"Now sit. You'll get the snake back after rehearsal."

"It belongs to Henry Jacobson."

It figured. Jack Frost had a wild side. Olivia only hoped the Mrs. could handle him.

"You sure you don't need help?" Walter asked, still standing before her. "You need a man around here."

"I'm not a damsel in distress, Mr. Brant. We're going to be fine." She smiled down at the twins. "Aren't we, boys?"

"Yes'm," Justin replied, sidling over to her while looking at his grandfather.

"Then you two go with Ms. Marshall," Walter

said, skepticism clouding his features. "I'll just go to the VFW and pick you up…" He looked at Olivia. "When?"

"I told Gabriel if you'd bring the boys, I'd walk them home. That was the deal."

"Deal?" Walter's brow furrowed further. "You two got something going on?"

"No!"

"Then why doesn't he want me to pick up the kids?"

"Perhaps he thought you could use a break. To be with your friends."

Walter harrumphed.

"Trust me," she said, although this man looked as if he trusted no one. "The boys are safe with me." She noticed that Regina had arrived, and Lynn was beginning to pass out song sheets to kids who were mostly seated and beginning to calm down. "I'd better go."

An afterthought made her turn back. "If you really want to help, we could use some extra candy-cane cutouts. Aunt Lydia used to say you were a woodworking wonder. Maybe you'd even like to help with scenery?"

"Now, let's not go overboard." Walter backed away. "Brants aren't exactly what you'd call joiners."

Olivia remembered a time—for a very short while—when Marjorie Brant had played piano for the high-school chorus. Now, she wondered if Walter had made his wife quit.

"No problem," she said with careful nonchalance, turning her attention to Lynn, who'd begun to explain to the children that today they would run through the songs and then they'd meet with Ms. Rollins to plan costumes. Justin and Jared clung to Olivia's cardigan. Her job, now, was to reassure these two boys rather than their intractable grandfather. It was always, after all, about the children.

Nonetheless, as she settled the twins beside her, she wondered how Gabriel, with all he had on his plate, was managing life alongside a man for whom discontent seemed to be a second skin.

WHILE MARMADUKE COOKED for the breakfast crowd, Gabriel left the stacks of flour tortillas and piles of chopped vegetables in his prep area, untied his apron, grabbed his windbreaker off the wall hook and pushed through the kitchen door into the dining room. Headed to the liquor store to pick up sherry for the vegetable wraps he'd planned for the special of the day, he should have been glad his boss was willing to let him slip out for ingredients not in the storeroom. But the sight of Walter coming into the diner, shaking off rain like an ill-tempered dog, soured Gabriel's mood. Maybe the old man was just stopping in for a cup of coffee.

That hope was dashed when Walter followed him outside.

Standing under the dripping awning, the two men eyed each other. Walter's breath rose in wisps on the chill air, as if the old man were some dragon just biding his time before he pounced. "You get fired?" he asked at last.

"I love the confidence you have in me."

"Well, did you?"

"No. I'm going to the liquor store. For sherry. For the lunch special." He hated that he'd given his father that much ammo.

"Sherry." Walter raised a pinky finger in the air. "Mac and cheese has come up in the world." He squinted at the rain. "Did you bring your car?"

"No." Gabriel was trying to save gas. Save money. Pinch pennies so he could get the hell out from under Walter's roof. From under his thumb.

"I'll drive you."

"It's only a couple blocks down Main."

"If you haven't noticed, the rain's coming down in buckets. The boys didn't give me an argument about driving the two blocks to the rec center. Kids have more sense than you. Get in the car."

Why the favor? Suspicious, Gabriel nonetheless thought about starting the lunch shift soaked to the skin—he needed to get himself more appropriate outerwear. "All right." The concession didn't mean he had to engage in conversation, however.

He'd forgotten about his dad's inclination to hold forth even if his listeners remained silent.

Inside the car, Walter quickly pulled out of the parking space. "I was headed to the VFW when I had a thought. You need a wife."

Gabriel let the slap of the windshield wipers fill the silence created by that bombshell.

"The boys need a mother," Walter added. Driving at a crawl, he fiddled with the defroster as the windows began to steam up. "And don't say they have a mother. That chippie's never gonna show her face again, and you know it."

"Morgana. Her name's Morgana and she's no 'chippie.'"

"Excuse me. Pole dancer. Does the distinction make her a better mother?"

"Just leave her out of it."

"That's what I'm trying to do. And you, because you actually had the good sense not to marry her, are free to get yourself a proper wife."

Thankfully, at this point, the liquor store came into view. Walter double-parked in front of the door. Gabriel couldn't get out of the car fast enough. After purchasing the sherry, he considered walking back to the diner, but the rain had turned into sleet. He didn't need to add pneumonia to his list of personal challenges. Besides, the guy Walter had blocked in was laying on his horn now.

Gabriel got back in the car, with Walter pulling away before he even had the door shut. The old man also made a U-turn right in the middle of Main Street.

"If you don't drive better than this when the twins are in the car," Gabriel warned, "they're not riding with you."

Walter rolled his eyes. "I know who'd make a perfect wife and mother. Olivia Marshall."

Gabriel struggled to get his seat belt unstuck without opening the door.

"It's the perfect solution," Walter continued. "The twins need a mother. Olivia needs to mother. Plus nothing seems to throw her off balance. I bet she wouldn't even bat an eye at your grouchiness."

"Oh, those are real good reasons to get married."

"Hey, in my parents' generation, need often came first. Then, if you were lucky, respect. If you were even luckier, love. Divorce statistics being what they are, I don't see your generation's made any great improvements in the process."

"I'm not looking to get married."

"You should be," Walter declared, as if years of marriage had made him a better man. Yeah, right. What kind of irascible SOB had he been before he'd met Marjorie? "Both of you should be. Don't know why Olivia isn't already settled down with a brood of her own. Nothin' wrong with the girl that I've heard of."

Olivia Marshall was none of Walter's business. None of Gabriel's, either.

As the diner came into view, Walter crossed the street to pull—the wrong way—into a spot right in front, even though a cop was coming down the sidewalk. In the future, the kids were never, ever riding with the old man.

"Think it over," Walter said, as Gabriel cata-
pulted from the car and slammed the door.

It wasn't even noon, and his brain was just about
fried from "thinking things over." He wished everyone would butt out of his affairs.

THE REHEARSAL ENDED much more smoothly than it
had begun. Song sheets had been distributed, and the
mostly familiar songs given a run-through. Olivia
had assigned each child a role, and then she, Lynn
and Regina had divided the children according to
roles, passing out simple costume instructions for the
parents. Next week, the children would run through
the songs again and learn some simple choreography.

During the entire rehearsal, Justin and Jared had
never left Olivia's side.

She realized that, for them, this morning had been
as daunting as the first day of class. Sure, today the
other kids—especially the ones who already knew
them—had made room for them without incident. In
all the bedlam, Jared's not talking wasn't an issue.
But if she was to provide appropriate stimulation in
order to jump-start his speech without overwhelming him, she was going to have to find a less hectic
environment. She didn't think Gabriel would approve
of her taking the boys to lunch before returning them
to Walter's. He'd probably see it as an act of charity.

But how could he object to a brief detour?

"Would you like to meet my parrot?" she asked
the twins as she helped them on with their jackets,

noting their outerwear was much more suitable for cold weather than Gabriel's had been at the Turkey Trot. Clearly, he put their needs first.

"You have a real parrot?" Justin asked.

"I sure do. His name is Burt, and he's an African gray."

"Does he talk?"

"So, you know about talking parrots?"

"The lady who lived in the other apartment above Daddy's restaurant had two parrots that talked. They flew away in the storm." The matter-of-fact way in which Justin talked about Hurricane Katrina, compared to Jared's silent obsession, sent a shiver through Olivia.

"Well, Burt talks," she replied. "A lot. He's had almost thirty-five years to learn to say many, many things. I already brought him to school earlier this year to meet my other students, so your meeting him now would be like catching up on your classwork."

"We wanna meet him!" Justin exclaimed, as Jared jiggled excitedly in agreement.

"Then we'll stop by my house on our way back to your grandpa's. I live right across the street from here."

It touched her how readily the two children slipped their hands into hers.

"Do you think we can run between the rain-drops?" she asked.

Justin gave her a superior look. "That's not possible!"

"Maybe, maybe not. When I use my imagination, anything's possible. Especially this time of year. Do you know what today is?"

"What?"

"December first. The beginning of Advent, the Christmas season."

"Santa and toys."

"Much more than that," she declared as she led the boys across the street to her house, where lights along the veranda railing twinkled a merry welcome. "It's the season of miracles!"

Olivia wholeheartedly believed what she said.

MARMADUKE STOPPED SERVING dinner at eight, and when Gabriel worked the night shift at the diner, he was home by nine. Tonight, he went upstairs to check on his sleeping sons before taking a quick shower to get rid of the food odors that stubbornly clung to his clothes and his hair. Only then did he go down to the kitchen, where he knew Walter would be drinking coffee and playing solitaire.

The old man looked extremely pleased with himself.

Although he wasn't hungry, Gabriel rummaged in the fridge for the milk and poured himself a glass, in an effort to stall whatever I-told-you-so moment was coming.

"I was right about Olivia Marshall," Walter said.

Oh, yeah. That.

"I'm tired," Gabriel replied, refusing to spar. "I think I'll turn in."

"Don't you want to know what happened with the boys today?"

"Of course." He just didn't want the telling liberally spiced with mentions of Olivia.

"I think Jared mighta had what shrinks call a breakthrough."

Gabriel put down the glass of milk with a thump that was hard enough to spill some of the contents. "Did he speak?"

"No. But he did something almost as good." Walter nodded toward the refrigerator, where the boys had been hanging their drawings.

There, amid Justin's fanciful portrayals of TV-perfect suburban landscapes, happy families and loyal dogs, and Jared's grim depictions of flood and loss, was a new picture with Jared's name scrawled in the corner. Three stick figures stood in a lush green, tropical setting. The people were clearly smiling. One figure—a woman, perhaps, judging from the long hair and standard triangle skirt—was holding a bird colored in remarkable detail. The body was gray, the tail red and the eyes a startling yellow. For two years now, Jared had used only three crayons. Blue. Black. Brown. This colorful drawing was a breakthrough, for sure.

"What happened at the rehearsal?" he asked.

"This wasn't from the rehearsal." Walter looked smug. "I told you Olivia was the best thing that could happen to the boys. After the rehearsal, she took them to her house, and—"

"Wait. She said if you'd take them to the rec center, she'd walk them home. Here, home. I didn't give her permission to take them to her house."

"Be glad she did. The boys met her parrot. When they got home, Justin couldn't stop talking about it, and Jared couldn't get at the crayons fast enough."

Gabriel was torn between an overwhelming sense of relief that Jared had recorded marked delight in something—anything—once again, and anger that Olivia couldn't seem to stop meddling.

"So, now what do you say about hooking up with your sons' teacher?" Walter asked, his jaw jutting out in challenge. "Seems like the perfect solution."

"When you're looking for a solution," Gabriel retorted, "it means you've got a problem. With all the things I might need right now, a wife isn't one of them."

Walter gave him a hard stare, but didn't say any more.

"Besides, I know next to nothing about Olivia Marshall. I shouldn't have let the boys go with her. For all I know, she's…"

"She's the closest thing to Mother Teresa Hennings has."

Why was that? Walter's statement stopped Gabriel in his tracks. Olivia was young, bright and attractive. Very attractive. So sue him for noticing.

Why was she still single? Devoted not to a husband and her own family but, seemingly selflessly, to Hennings's endless batches of kindergarteners?

Gabriel didn't trust "selfless." At best, the trait was hopelessly naive, and at worst, manipulative.

He didn't care about Olivia's marital status. He cared about her interference—in his own family matters—and he had to put a stop to the meddling. Although he was dead on his feet, he had to do it now. Throwing his soggy jacket back on, he stormed out of the house and into the needle-sharp rain.

CHAPTER SIX

THE RAIN ON THE solarium's tin roof, the pitch-black winter night beyond the windows and the fire in the living-room fireplace made Olivia sleepy, although it wasn't yet ten-thirty. Twice she'd dozed off over her book and had awakened in her armchair to find that Burt—free from his cage for his evening flight—had gotten into mischief.

"Bad weather," the parrot muttered from his perch on the fireplace mantel, where he was shredding a Christmas card. "Burt wants towel game." The towel game was a simple snuggling exercise that calmed Burt when he was uneasy or insecure. "Olivia, please, get the gray towel!" he ordered in perfect mimicry of Aunt Lydia's voice. "Not the striped. Burt doesn't like the striped."

Olivia chuckled. African grays were arguably the most intelligent birds on the planet. Not only could they mimic with uncanny precision and store up and retrieve a vocabulary that would make the most prolific writer envious, they could then retool that mimicry and that vocabulary into original utterances. Scientists were slowly beginning to admit that African grays could do more than just "parrot." They could talk. And talk. And *talk,* in Burt's case. Aunt Lydia had bought the young bird years before Olivia had come to live with them, and had spent long hours teaching her willing pupil.

Olivia stood, then approached the mantel, holding out her hand to Burt. "Step up, please."

The parrot cocked his head suspiciously. "Towel game."

"Yes. Towel game. Then bed."

He stepped onto her hand. "Kiss Burt."

"How do you ask?"

"Pretty please."

Olivia kissed his beak and stroked his neck as she carefully made her way through the French doors into the plant-filled solarium where she kept his cage.

Burt eyed the cage dubiously. "Towel game," he warned.

"Towel game," she agreed, settling herself on a stool by the cage and picking up one of the many gray towels Burt accepted as a kind of surrogate mother. For several minutes she allowed him his game of hide and seek, a game of which he never tired. Finally, she offered him the open cage door.

"A nightcap would be nice," he said in Aunt Lydia's voice, before settling on his perch to lull himself with a perfect imitation of the rain on the roof.

Olivia took a dried apricot from a sealed container, bit into it and ate half, then shared the other half with Burt.

"Sleep well," she said, lowering the night sheet over the cage.

"Bed bugs bite," he muttered in response.

Olivia had put the fireplace screen in position and turned out all the lights except the one on the porch when a thunderous knocking began at the front door, causing Burt to squawk loudly.

Who was out in this nasty weather? Hurrying down the hallway, she could see through the sidelights a figure—Gabriel, of all people—standing on the porch in his insubstantial hooded windbreaker. His expression was darker than the rain-drenched night.

"Come in!" she exclaimed, throwing open the door. "Did you walk? You're soaked through! Let's get you dry."

"Stop!"

"Stop what?"

"Stop your damned good works. Stop your interfering. Stop your mothering."

Mothering. With a sinking heart, she thought of Justin and Jared. "Are the boys all right?"

"They're fine." For a minute Gabriel looked confused, as if he'd forgotten why he'd come. Then a shadow passed across his rugged features. "That's why I'm here. To tell you they're fine—*we're* fine—without any help from you." He was dripping on the doormat.

"We can discuss this like adults," she insisted, pulling him inside the foyer and quelling the hurt that came with his constant brusqueness. This shouldn't be about her. It wasn't even about an old friendship, which she was beginning to doubt had ever existed. It was about what was best for Justin and Jared. Her students. "Take off that jacket and come in by the fire. I won't accept no for an answer."

She turned around and marched back into the living room, sure that whatever argument he'd come to pick would spur him to follow. Her professional armor in place, she was up for the encounter.

When he did follow, she noticed he'd unzipped his jacket, but he didn't look as if he intended to take it off or stay.

"Hang your coat on that wooden chair," she suggested as she added sticks and stoked the fire.

"You're a bossy woman," Gabriel declared, his anger barely contained.

"Bossy woman," came the muttered echo from the solarium.

"My parrot," she explained, lest Gabriel think they were being eavesdropped on by some multiple-personality roommate. "And both of you are out of line. He's already in his cage. Do you need a little time-out, as well?" If Gabriel was going to behave like a schoolboy, she'd treat him like one.

"I'm here to tell you *you* were out of line with the detour you took with my sons this afternoon. To meet your parrot. *Without my permission.*"

Why was he so upset? In the flickering firelight, she stared into his beautiful but cold blue eyes and felt dismay at the extent of his inexplicable anger. "Justin and Jared seemed to enjoy the visit. Very much, in fact. Was there a problem once they got home?"

"No. But I shouldn't have let you be part of the care system Walter and I have worked out."

"Why not?"

"You're their teacher. Stick to teaching them the basics. In school. Outside class, I'm capable of providing enrichment activities for my sons."

"If that's the kind of cold and compartmentalized life you wanted, you shouldn't have returned to Hennings. It might sound corny or outdated, but we still live by the adage 'It takes a village to raise a child.'"

He shivered.

She wouldn't ask him again to take off that wet jacket. Instead, she reached out to lift it from his shoulders.

With lightning swiftness he grasped her wrist. His bare hand was icy cold. "Always part teacher, part social worker," he growled. "You don't give up, do you?"

She pulled away from him, tugging his jacket off at the same time and hanging it on the chair near the fireplace. He couldn't know how his barb had hit the mark. How being "professional" was part of her emotional protection.

"What is your problem?" she asked, turning the question back on him. "People have been nothing but nice to you since you came back to town, yet you've been a complete bear." To her, in particular. "Why is that?"

"The short answer?" he asked, stretching his hands toward the fire. "I don't like people sticking their noses in my business."

"Then why did you come back to such a small community? Sticking our noses in other people's business is what we do best. It's called looking out for each other. Lending a helping hand."

"I don't need help."

His rigid stance said otherwise. She couldn't picture anyone else she knew in greater need of basic TLC, but she held her tongue.

"My family doesn't need handouts," he declared, the muscle along his jaw rippling.

The rain beat a staccato rhythm on the roof. The wood again crackled cheerily in the fireplace. From underneath his night sheet in the solarium, Burt softly whistled the overture to *West Side Story*. All the while, this wet and intractable man stood before her, scowling like the Grinch. She stifled inappropriate laughter.

"You think this is funny?" he asked, his tone biting. "Is this a game to you?"

"No," she replied, seriously. "As to the parrot, all my students meet Burt. I'd already brought him to school for our rain forest unit earlier this fall. By bringing Justin and Jared to meet him today, I was striving to include them in our little classroom community. Inclusion is going to be a big part in healing their hurt." And Gabriel's hurt, too, she guessed.

"Outside the classroom," he said, his anger still simmering just below the surface, "don't take matters into your own hands. Before involving my boys, I want you to ask my permission. Do you understand?"

"Yes." In a startling moment of insight, she understood this wasn't about a parrot at all. It wasn't even about her, personally. It was about control. For twenty-seven months this strong man, in reduced circumstances, had been trying to regain control of his life. She could only imagine the frustration she might feel in his place.

How could she begin to penetrate the layers of his protective shell? Gabriel needed kindness, that was for sure, and kindness she could give. Instinctively, she reached out her hand to cup his cheek, and felt more than the mere human connection she'd wished to communicate.

She felt his skin, still cold and wet from the elements—and something more. She felt an unmistakable spark. A culmination of all the longing and restlessness that had been her constant companions these past couple of weeks.

Gabriel tried to step back from Olivia's touch, but he found he couldn't. His feet seemed nailed to the floor. Bathed in firelight, she was looking at him with those big brown eyes, which said—way too clearly—she expected something from him. Something he knew he couldn't supply. But was it as a father or as a man? His nostrils flared involuntarily as he smelled a trap.

"Gabriel," she said, so softly he almost thought he'd imagined it. Imagined, too, the jolt the sound of his name on her lips gave him.

This was crazy. He could not be attracted to this woman. The only link he had with her was through his kids. And that innocent time years ago when they'd been kids themselves.

"I'm not the enemy," she continued in a near whisper, her hand still on his cheek. Scorching him.

He reached up, determined to break the all-too-powerful connection he felt. This heat. This surprising and unreasonable desire. Instead of brushing her away, however, he pressed her hand more closely to his flesh. As if he couldn't get enough of her touch. Her warmth. As if his hand had a mind of its own.

"I'm only passing through Hennings," he said, his words a rasp as he struggled to free himself of an inexplicable hunger.

"That remains to be seen," she breathed, her pupils dilating as if she was surprised by her own words. As if she, too, felt somehow possessed.

Except for the fire, the room was dark. The rain drumming on the roof and against the windows seemed to create a barrier, separating them from the outside world. The real world. What was happening here in this room wasn't real. That was for damn sure.

Why he did what he did next, he'd never know. Maybe he wanted to see if he was dreaming and would wake up, the more absurd the dream became. Maybe he wanted to play the big-city rat and scare off the sweet little country mouse. Maybe he wanted to see the stuff she was really made of.

Or maybe—for whatever crazy reason—he just wanted her.

Whatever. The night had already gone so far beyond his control he couldn't be held responsible for any more craziness. He pulled her to him and kissed her hard.

And she kissed him back. With a stunning passion that swept away the last of his restraint.

Life had served up nothing but cold, bitter dishes lately, and her lips were so sweet, her hands so soft on his skin, driving him to distraction. He buried his face in her neck and heard her sigh. *Don't make this so easy for me,* he thought, even as he drew her closer. A man could take only so much temptation. A starving man could take none at all.

He ran his hands over her body. Who wouldn't, in his situation? She was offering—why, he couldn't guess, but what red-blooded man could resist? Her supple curves. The way her body moved with his, to charge the air with pure need. With absolute want.

They were standing, fully clothed, but Gabriel felt as if there was nothing between them.

Olivia drew him toward the sofa. Pulled him down on top of her. Kissed his lips. Nipped his tongue. Stroked his back. Stoked his ego. Broke through the wall he'd built around himself. Made him drop his guard and forget to look for potential traps. Made him think that for a few moments he could steal some physical comfort for himself.

She was willing. He could tell. In fact, her response told him she'd been denying herself in some way, too. And that she needed to let go of that deprivation.

He slid his hand under her sweater to the warm bare skin beneath. Wrapping her arms tightly around his shoulders, she trailed tiny, electrifying kisses along his jaw.

The dark, pierced only by the firelight, and the icy rain rattling the windows, drove any remaining shred of the outside world away. Privacy—of which he'd had none these past two years—was a powerful aphrodisiac.

Olivia moved Gabriel's hand to her breast. He felt her nipple strain against the lacy fabric of her bra, as he strained against the impulse to take her. Now. Fast. Before they came to their senses.

Instead, he lost himself in kissing her mouth. Her hot, delicious mouth. This wasn't the demure kindergarten teacher he'd found when he'd come back to town. This was the adventurous, swing-for-the-fences individual of years ago. For the first time in months and months, as Gabriel explored her body, he felt heat begin to return to his limbs.

He slid his hand inside the waistband of her slacks. Found the moist warmth between her legs. She gasped and arched against him. As he caressed her, he felt all the old anger inside him begin to dissolve. She smelled so damn good. So powdery soft and feminine, with a hint of wanton desire. He could lose himself in this woman.

She reached for the buckle on his belt.

Looking into her eyes, he heard her name echo in his head: *Olivia.* Not a means to an end, but a real woman. And not just any woman, but a woman his father had said should have marriage and a family. A commitment. In this town, where she already had roots.

Suddenly, it was if he'd taken a plunge in a frigid lake.

"What's wrong?" she asked softly, her breathing heavy.

"We can't do this." He sat up, trying not to be drawn into the hurt in her eyes. "For a million reasons."

"Give me one."

"As I said before, I'm not staying in Hennings."

"That has nothing to do with tonight."

"It has everything to do with tonight. You're no one-night stand," he said with conviction. And he couldn't deal with anything more than a one-night stand.

Olivia felt cold wash over her. It wasn't just that the flames in the fireplace had burned low again. It wasn't just the absence of Gabriel's touch. She felt as if a door had been closed in her face, after she'd had the chance to see through the crack. Seen the other side, where the answer to all her nameless longings beckoned. Now here she was, shut out. Not for the first time in her life. On the outside, not even looking in anymore.

Her body ached.

"We're both adults," she said, even as the reality hit her. She'd almost made love to the father of two of her students. She'd almost stopped playing by the rules.

"Adults?" he asked, his tone skeptical. "Irresponsible adults, it would seem." Still sitting on the edge of the sofa, he looked down at her, his expression unreadable. "I'm not carrying any protection. What about you?"

"No," she admitted. What had come over them? Over her? Sitting up, she self-consciously smoothed her hair and then her clothing. A few moments ago she'd wanted this man more than she'd wanted anyone, anything, in a long, long while. It pained her to admit to herself that she *still* wanted him. What had happened to her personal mantra, which revolved around the word *should?*

The wind howled outside, hurling the rain against the house in angry blasts. If she could only blame her rash behavior on the storm…

"I'm sorry," he said.

"You are?"

"Yeah," he replied almost sheepishly. "You're my kids' teacher."

He couldn't have said anything worse. Anything that would make her feel more guilty. Or more marginalized. Objectified. Less like a woman.

"Of course." She was trying for detached. Worldly-wise. Instead, she sounded schoolmarmish. She stood and wondered, briefly, if her legs would even support her. Reaching for the end table, she nearly tipped over a potted poinsettia that she'd so carefully picked out just this afternoon. Ironically, *careful* didn't seem to be a part of her vocabulary at the moment.

"Look…"

"I was as much to blame as you," she said. "We both lost our heads. Why, I have no idea. But it won't happen again. And it's forgotten already." She handed him his soggy windbreaker. "I'll show you out."

At the front door he turned to her. "Olivia…"

"You know, maybe it would be better if we stuck to Ms. Marshall. Since I'm your sons' teacher."

Something in him seemed to harden. "Sure."

A blast of damp air hit her as Gabriel opened the door. Before she could soften the hurtful thing she'd said, he disappeared into the night.

She closed the door, then slumped against it. All the lovely sensuality of moments earlier, all the desire, all the heat drained from her. Replaced not by remorse, but by a profound emptiness.

"Someone's been a very naughty girl," Burt

called from his cage in the solarium, in a spot-on imitation of the villain in his favorite soap opera.

It hit Olivia that her emptiness came not from being a naughty girl tonight, but from the fact that she'd rarely, if ever, strayed into naughty-girl territory until now. Before tonight, she'd worn her integrity as a badge. Now she wondered if it wasn't merely part of her armor.

Protecting her against risk. Against the unknown. Against attachment. And loss.

CHAPTER SEVEN

OLIVIA AWOKE Sunday morning with the feeling she'd had one too many margaritas. Who knew acting wildly irresponsible—even without alcohol—could give you a hangover?

She pulled the covers over her head at the thought of her behavior the night before. Not at the idea of almost having mad, passionate sex on her sofa in front of the fire. No, that thought wasn't what made her burrow deeper under the duvet. It was the memory of herself standing at the front door after Gabriel's departure…wishing he'd return.

Was she certifiably mad?

In how many ways was her overwhelming attraction to this man a bad idea?

One: he was the father of two of her students. Two: he was a man who made no bones about moving on when the opportunity presented itself. Three: he was an angry man, who seemed not soothed by her presence, but provoked by it.

What made her want to throw herself in his path?

He wasn't even the same person she'd been friends with in childhood.

Her bedside alarm rang. If she didn't get up now, she'd be late for the brunch at which she and Lynn and Regina had planned to meet with the volunteer musicians for the children's pageant. She had to be there.

Reluctantly, she crawled out of bed and headed for the bathroom. As she brushed her teeth, she avoided her reflection in the mirror.

Oh, you big chicken!

She spat out toothpaste, then forced herself to stare straight ahead into her own eyes. Forced herself to take in the hair that hadn't seen an updated style in ages, the thermal underwear she wore as pajamas and the well-scrubbed girl-next-door demeanor that screamed, "I'm nice!" And at that moment she knew why she'd almost had unprotected sex last night with a near stranger.

If she didn't add a little variety to her life, a little excitement—a little danger, even—she was going to lose her mind.

There, she'd admitted it.

Mortified at the admission, she threw on her black tights, her black high-heeled boots, her little black pencil skirt and her black cashmere turtleneck. And sighed. This was her sophisticated weekend look. Her break from serviceable kindergarten tops and trousers. It wasn't exactly, she thought ruefully, an outfit to jump-start an adventure.

But it was too late to change. Her clothes, anyway. Besides, she knew it wasn't her hair or her wardrobe that had her chomping at the bit. And it wasn't really her life. She loved her life. It just needed a little spicing up. Dare she say it? It needed the likes of Gabriel Brant. Only with condoms on hand the next time.

SUNDAY, the diner was closed, which gave the entire staff the day off. Standing at Walter's kitchen sink before the rest of the household awoke, Gabriel mentally spent his Saturday paycheck. He'd allocated it to his credit card debt and to some upcoming expenses for the boys. Yet it wasn't this thought or the overcast day he beheld through the small curtained window that had him so gloomy.

It was Olivia Marshall, and the fact he'd wanted her last night more than he'd wanted anything in recent memory. Talk about unrealistic expectations.

"Daddy, will you make pancakes for breakfast?" Justin appeared in the doorway, yawning.

"I will." Gabriel pulled himself out of his state of self-absorption. "Where's Jared?"

"He's in the living room. Drawing a picture of Ms. Marshall's parrot. We wanna go see it again today."

"Do you know where your grandfather is?" Gabriel asked, rummaging in the cupboards for supplies and utensils, and deliberately dodging Justin's request. Visiting Olivia was the very last thing he'd consider doing today.

"Grampa went out."

"And now he's back," Walter declared, striding into the kitchen with several large McDonald's bags. "With breakfast."

"I was going to make pancakes," Gabriel replied, unable to keep the bite out of his words.

"So, I already bought Mickey D's." Walter placed the bags on the table. "How 'bout you, Justin? You think you could choke down a couple Egg McMuffins?"

"Yes, sir!"

"Then go get your brother."

When Justin left the room, Walter stopped unloading the contents of the bags to give Gabriel a crooked grin. "How'd your confrontation with Olivia go last night? You were pretty damned riled up when you left the house, but I'm betting she can hold her own. I'd like to have been a fly on the wall." He appeared less like a fly and more like a spider contemplating the prey caught in its web. "So, did you put her in her place or did she put you in yours?"

Washing up at the sink, Gabriel didn't answer his father.

"I hope you watched your language, 'cause I hear tell that parrot of hers can repeat anything, and I mean anything—conversations, sounds, voices—after hearing it just once."

The boys barreled into the kitchen. "See, I told you," Justin crowed. "Mickey D's!"

As the twins scrambled into their seats, Gabriel thought of Olivia and the craziness of the night before. As much as he'd wanted her, he couldn't be sidetracked by more than a fling. And as he'd said to her, she deserved more. Maybe retreat, on his part, was the better part of valor. He really needed to ratchet up his search for a better paying job.

But then he looked at Justin and Jared gobbling their breakfast in the kitchen of his childhood. The twins—including Jared—had actually seemed happy in the two weeks since their arrival in Hennings. They liked living at Grampa Walter's, and, God only knew why, Walter seemed to relish his role as grandfather—even though he still didn't seem to have a handle on fatherhood. Gabriel had brought his sons home to heal, and they'd begun to do just that. And no matter that he tried to deny it, Walter— and Olivia—had played a big part in the boys' first steps toward recovery.

In all good conscience, Gabriel couldn't move them again right now.

He just needed to avoid Olivia. With his work schedule and Walter's willingness to help with the school routine, it shouldn't be too difficult to stay out of her way.

Out of temptation's way.

"OLIVIA!" Kelly called as Olivia checked her school mailbox early Monday morning before classes began. "Do you know you're wearing two different shoes?"

Olivia looked down at her feet. She was losing it. Always organized, she'd often secretly tut-tutted when other teachers dragged themselves in at the beginning of the week, scattered or clearly ill-prepared.

"It's for a 'mismatch' story I plan to do with the kids," she replied hastily, as she pulled the contents out of her mailbox.

Amid ads for surefire reading programs and fund-raisers, there was a red paper bag decorated with holly and filled with chocolates. From her Secret Santa. Olivia suppressed a groan. The first week in December was the kickoff for this behind-the-scenes faculty activity, which *she* organized each year. *She'd* had every intention of baking cookies yesterday for her secret pal, but instead she'd spent Sunday in a Gabriel-Brant-induced fog. For goodness sake, she wasn't a moon-eyed adolescent. She needed to get a grip—and fast.

"Olivia?" Elyse Gilbert, the school-district psychologist, stood in front of her. "Do you have a minute?"

"Sure, if you'll walk with me to my classroom." Olivia always liked to get to school an hour before the kids in order to center herself and make sure she was totally prepared before the day began. Today, after her unsettling weekend, she needed the extra time more than ever. "Is this about Jared Brant's tests?"

"Yes," Elyse replied, waiting until they were in the privacy of Olivia's classroom before she elaborated.

"I want to thank you for putting a rush on his evaluation," Olivia said. Elyse headed a team that administered hearing, sight, physical coordination and psychological evaluations to all incoming students. Olivia had pressed Elyse to move Jared's appointment to the top of their list. "He's a special little boy."

"He is. And even considering what you told me about his Katrina experience, I think he's going to be fine. We were concerned about possible hearing problems, but he checked out okay in that area, as in all the others. He's bright and curious. I think his not speaking will eventually work itself out."

"So do I. But do you have any suggestions for hastening the process?"

"I have one. And I wanted to run it by you before we meet with Mr. Brant." Elyse, who recognized Olivia's devotion to her students, eyed her cautiously. "What do you think of separating the twins? Of putting one of them in Megan's class."

"Oh, no! Why would you want to do that?"

"Because, as you say, Justin does all the talking for his brother, so that Jared doesn't need to speak for himself."

"But twins have such a special bond."

"That's exactly why it's so easy for Justin to communicate Jared's needs. Jared really needs to communicate for himself."

The thought of giving up one of the boys made Olivia sad. How could she choose? "Even with

Justin speaking for him," she countered, "Jared made noticeable gains in just one week. By Friday, it was obvious he wanted to be right in the middle of all our activities, and when I took the boys home to meet Burt on Saturday—"

"You took the boys to your house?"

"On the way back from the winterfest rehearsal. Because their father works Saturday, their grandfather's going to bring them to rehearsal and I'm going to walk them to their house."

Elyse looked doubtful. "Do you have a previous personal relationship with the family?"

"Not really. But Gabriel...their father doesn't seem eager to enroll them in any extracurricular activities. Which I think would go a long way to helping Jared's speech. Then, their grandfather, who's acting as babysitter, seems to think that jaunts to the VFW are adequate stimulation."

"Olivia," Elyse replied, her voice well modulated, careful. "We found no indication of neglect or mistreatment with either of these boys."

"I'm not suggesting that! But I think stimulation and enrichment would go a long way in getting Jared to open up. And I think the two men are stretched to their limit."

"Perhaps. But you should work your magic within the school day." Elyse placed her hand on Olivia's arm. "The rest is up to the family. If they need help, they can ask."

"Not likely. The Brants are proud men. They obviously want what's best for Justin and Jared, but these children have gone without for over two years. Did you know this is their first school experience?"

"I didn't. But as I said, Jared appears to be extremely bright. Obviously, their father has done his best to engage the twins." Elyse's response seemed measured, even though the two women had been friends outside of work for years. "I know you want the best for all your students. Your district evaluations every year have been stellar. But Olivia, you have to draw the line. You're a teacher. Not a social worker. Not your students' mother."

"I know." This wasn't the first time friends had cautioned her about becoming emotionally involved in her students' welfare. "But in Justin and Jared's situation, there isn't a mother present."

Elyse gave her an appraising glance, and said nothing. Olivia suspected her colleague was weighing the possibility that she and Gabriel had already been thrown together by the local matchmakers. Olivia wished she could deny any connection to the father and state categorically that the boys' educational welfare was her only concern, their education her only goal. She wanted what was best for their development. Absolutely, they should be a separate issue from their father. But their father... Now there was the sticking point.

"What's going on, Olivia?"

"I admit my heart goes out to these boys." She took

a deep breath. "Even though I don't want to see them split up at school, I'll defer to your judgment and their father's wishes. Have you set up a conference?"

"Not yet. I wanted to make sure you and I were on the same page first. I'll get back to you after I contact Mr. Brant."

Olivia felt deflated after Elyse left the classroom. On Friday, she would have sworn her motives in regard to the twins were absolutely professional. But after Saturday night? What was really happening? *Tick-tock, tick-tock.* Was that merely her classroom clock reminding her that her students would be arriving shortly…or her biological clock making its presence felt?

Was she guilty of seeing a ready-made family and positioning herself to benefit?

Ouch. That made her seem desperate.

In an effort to summon her self-control, she lifted her take-home tote onto her desk and searched fruitlessly for her lesson plan book. It simply wasn't there. How could she have left that most important of teachers' tools at home? In ten years on the job, she hadn't ever begun a Monday in such a distracted state.

"What the hell's a turducken?" Marmaduke asked, as he read the Monday dinner special Gabriel was chalking onto the board behind the counter.

"It's a Cajun delicacy. A boneless chicken, stuffed inside a boneless duck, stuffed inside a boneless turkey. There won't be any leftovers, trust me."

"Oh, I trust you. Each time you cooked, last week, we sold out of all the specials—lunch and dinner." Marmaduke scratched his head. "I gotta tell you, you're bringing in a whole different crowd."

"Is that bad?"

"No. The regulars are still showing up—some are even deviating from the usual to try your new stuff. You're good, that's all I'm saying."

"Thanks." Positive feedback was always welcome. Not as welcome as running his own restaurant would be, but Gabriel recognized a decent start when he saw one. "I'm going to take my meal break now."

Marmaduke would spell him if anyone ordered from the regular menu, although most of the mid-afternoon trade revolved around coffee and pastry, and it was mostly takeout, at that. His boss didn't move toward the kitchen, however. "That phone call you got earlier. Anything you want to talk about?"

"No. It was the school again." He didn't want to say *the school psychologist,* even though that's who it had been. "Jared's having a little trouble adjusting. He'll be okay." But not if the school separated the twins. He knew that much.

He headed into the kitchen, where he made himself a sandwich, and then took it to the farthest booth in a corner of the dining room. Sat with his face to the wall. Marmaduke took the hint and left him alone.

The school psychologist—a Dr. Gilbert—had really wanted to set up an appointment to discuss Jared's entry evaluation. But when she'd said Olivia would be involved, he'd pleaded the difficulty of getting away from work during school hours, and had convinced Dr. Gilbert to give him her report and recommendation over the phone. She—and apparently Olivia, too—wanted to separate the twins. Actually, he wouldn't have minded the idea of transferring both boys out of Olivia's classroom, minimizing his own contact with her, but Dr. Gilbert had insisted a move like that would defeat the purpose. He'd insisted he didn't want his sons split up. End of discussion.

So why did the whole issue keep replaying itself in his head?

He was startled to realize he'd eaten his sandwich without even tasting it. He needed to focus. Distractions were dangerous in a kitchen. And Olivia had become a major distraction. Olivia? It had been Dr. Gilbert who'd contacted him. But Gabriel wondered if Olivia had been behind the call. Why would she have been? In retaliation for Saturday night? Even with the coincidence of the Monday call, he couldn't quite bring himself to see her as that petty.

What was he to think? To do?

Hell, he'd already done it. He'd told Dr. Gilbert the twins were to stay together. Now, he needed to minimize his contact with Olivia. He'd like to know, however, just how he was going to juggle his own best interests and also maintain his sons'.

The diner door opened, setting off a tinny version of "Have a Holly, Jolly Christmas." The waitresses had been going crazy with the decorations, and he'd put a crick in his neck dodging the mistletoe that seemed to hang everywhere.

"Hi, Maggie!" Olivia called out. Even with his back turned, he knew her voice. The last voice he wanted to hear. "Can I get a coffee and a raspberry tart to go?"

Call him a coward, but Gabriel never turned around. It was better to let go of the past. Tread lightly in the present and focus on the future.

When he arrived at Walter's later that night after work, however, the past reared up to bite him on the butt.

Walter and the boys were already in bed and asleep, but an envelope addressed to Gabriel sat propped against the saltshaker on the kitchen table. Although there was no return address, he recognized the distinctive, childish scrawl. Morgana's.

After four years and not a single word from her, he was convinced she'd left the boys with him for good. All he had, though, in the way of anything resembling official custody was his name on their birth certificates. He wanted legal custody. But to get it, he'd have to track down their mother. He'd used the Internet in various public libraries, and over the years he'd managed to come up with several different addresses, but nothing more. He'd written to each of them, the most recent time including his plans to move back to Hennings, plus his father's address as a contact.

Suddenly nervous about her response, he eyed the postmark. Tulsa, Oklahoma. He ripped open the envelope and read the enclosed message. "I'm glad to hear you and the boys survived Katrina. I want to talk to you about them, but I think we ought to do it face-to-face. If you wire me bus fare, I can come to New York. I've never seen snow."

Snow? She hadn't seen her sons in four years, and all she could mention was the prospect of seeing snow?

He wanted legal custody of his sons, yeah, but how close was he willing to let this woman get in the process?

CHAPTER EIGHT

WAS IT SAFE TO DO what she was about to do?

Olivia tightened the grip on her tote bag and continued along the sidewalk toward Walter Brant's house. A week without running into Gabriel had given her time to regain her composure and convince herself she was once again operating in purely professional fashion. And, yes, this errand was necessary. More than necessary, in fact—it was a rather brilliant idea. Besides, she *and* Lynn had come up with it on the phone last night, after the second pageant practice, and Lynn had asked, pretty please, if Olivia could carry it out because she had her hands full with three kids who were waiting to be taken to Grandma's for Christmas cookie making.

So, a pesky little voice in Olivia's head asked, *why did you wait to run this "errand" on Sunday, when you know the diner is closed and Gabriel will be free? Hmm?*

"Shut up!" she said to herself aloud, startling an elderly couple who were dressed to the nines and obviously fresh from church. All she needed was for someone to report to her principal that they'd seen formerly dependable Ms. Marshall wandering along Winterberry Street, mumbling incoherently to herself.

She smiled at the pair and began to hum "I'll Be Home for Christmas," then stopped. Humming to oneself might not be perceived as a lot saner than mumbling.

Maybe her repatched professional veneer was cracking. Maybe seven days without seeing Gabriel wasn't quite enough recovery time. Recovery? She wasn't sick. Well, she did have an upset stomach from eating her own cooking all week. Usually, the diner functioned as her second kitchen, but Monday afternoon, when she'd stopped in for coffee and a raspberry tart, she'd seen Gabriel sitting in the corner booth, his back to the world and his shoulders stiff, as if they needed a good massage—and she gave really, really great shoulder rubs… She'd begun thinking about Saturday night, and then she'd found herself standing in front of the cash register with Maggie commenting on how it must be awfully cold outside, judging by Olivia's bright red cheeks. She knew then she needed to stay away from the diner.

And maybe, too, she needed to stay away from Walter Brant's house.

"I hope you're not as lost as you look." Walter himself, Christmas tree stand in hand, was walking from his garage down his driveway. "You just passing by, or you here to see Gabriel and the boys?"

His mouth quirked in a lopsided grin, as if he wasn't used to the motion. "I know you're not here to see an old fart—excuse my French—like me."

"Ah…actually." She couldn't recall completing the two and a half blocks from her house to his. "I wanted to see all of you."

"Come on in." Walter waited for her to climb the porch steps. "We're putting up the tree."

"In that case, I shouldn't interrupt."

"Nonsense. A Christmas tree needs a woman's eye." He paused before opening the front door. "I haven't put one up since Marjorie…" He let the words trail off. "Anyway, I thought the kids would like one."

Olivia hesitated.

"We won't bite," he said, actually looking as if he might.

Okay. This was a really, really quick and uncomplicated errand.

When Walter opened the door to let her through first, Olivia could see the twins playing in an empty cardboard box while Gabriel sorted through what looked like extremely old and moth-eaten sections of an artificial Christmas tree.

"Walter," he said, "this is a piece of crap."

Walter cleared his throat. "Lady present."

Gabriel turned slowly.

"Ms. Marshall!" Justin crowed. "Look at our pirate ship! When Dad puts up the tree, we're gonna look for buried treasure under it."

"I think this tree's treasure days are over," Gabriel stated sourly, holding up one spindly branch.

"Shake it," Walter ordered. "It'll fluff out."

Gabriel shook it—and most of the fake needles flew off.

"If I could make a suggestion…" Olivia thought this tree the most pitiful, most unholidaylike thing she'd ever seen. "The community center is selling real trees. All sizes. All prices. And the proceeds will go toward next year's children's pageant. They're even open today."

Gabriel didn't bite, but Walter's eyes seemed to light up. "Whadya say, boys? Would you like to put a real tree in the house? I'll spring for it."

Jared giggled. "Real trees don't fit in the house, Grampa," Justin said.

"Well, we'll see about that. Get your coats. Hats and mittens, too. Ms. Marshall's going to help pick out a Christmas tree."

As the boys scampered out of the room, Gabriel cut a hard glance at his father, then Olivia. "Was this prearranged?"

"No!" Olivia replied emphatically as Walter made himself busy cleaning up the mess produced by the artificial tree. "I came over here because I wanted to give Jared something."

"Just Jared?" Gabriel didn't seem pleased.

"Actually, after observing the kids at the pageant rehearsal yesterday, Lynn and I decided on a few minor changes." Olivia pulled a child's recorder and a sheet of simple music out of her tote. "At school, Jared loves the rhythm instruments we use. And at yesterday's rehearsal he kept wandering from his group, which was supposed to be practicing 'The Friendly Beasts,' with Ty Mackey's animals, over to the 'Frosty the Snowman' group, which has adult musicians. When I saw that musical instruments trumped the prospect of live animals, I thought he'd be great in the children's recorder chorus. He gets to keep the recorder."

"I don't know," Gabriel replied.

"He seems to have a real interest. It's not a lot to learn. Just a few notes. The fingering's drawn for you here." She held out the sheet music. "I know he can do it."

"Why not Justin, too?"

"Because he really loves the idea of performing with live animals. He's fine right where he is." She suspected Gabriel might think that, to be fair, both boys should have received a recorder—or neither. "You know, deep down I didn't think the boys should be split up at school, but they don't need to do everything in lockstep. They're twins, yes, but they're also individuals."

Putting the last of the artificial tree parts into the cardboard box, Walter muttered something under his breath.

"I beg your pardon?" Even though Walter wasn't the twins' father, Olivia recognized that since these four were all living under the same roof, it would be better for the boys if their grandfather felt part of the process.

"I said I don't want you turning my grandson into one of those wimpy orchestra boys," he murmured, only slightly louder this time.

Olivia bristled. "Mr. Brant, I won't have anyone limiting—or labeling—my students. Not even a grandfather. You need to stop and think, before your grandsons hear you and wonder if you put conditions on your love. Moreover, if Jared does prove to have musical ability, don't you imagine Marjorie would have been proud as anything?"

Walter backed down and actually appeared to mull over her words, whereas Gabriel just stared, the corners of his mouth twitching. In irritation, agreement or amusement?

"We're ready!" Justin and Jared ran back into the room, trailing their coats behind them. They moved so in sync, their expressions so similar, and Justin's declarations always so inclusive, that sometimes it almost seemed as if Jared had spoken.

"I'll get our coats." Gabriel looked pointedly at Walter. "Is yours in the back entry?"

"Oh, I'm not going," his dad replied, beginning to help the boys put on their outerwear. "The Bills are playing the Dolphins. I can't miss that."

Gabriel looked as if he might back out, as well, until he glanced at his sons' eager faces. "Hold on." Still holding Jared's recorder and the sheet music, he left the room with a glare at his father.

"Mr. Brant," Olivia hazarded. "If you're not coming because of me… If you feel insulted—"

"I don't. I like a plainspoken woman. And call me Walter. I feel old enough as it is, without the 'mister' handle."

"Ms. Marshall?" Justin tugged on her coat. "We want to visit your parrot."

She'd already gotten in deeper this afternoon than she'd intended to. "You know, I've been thinking the other children might like that, too. I should bring Burt to school again, so everyone in class can see him. Good idea?"

Both boys nodded vigorously.

"Tomorrow, then."

Walter had finished putting all the pieces of the old tree back in the cardboard box and was now carefully taping it shut, as if he thought he might still have use for it in the future. "Don't get a scrawny tree," he admonished, when Gabriel came back into the room. As if anything could be worse than the poor misfit he'd just boxed up. Such care for a object and such dismissiveness toward his own son left Olivia saddened.

"Why don't you come with us and pick it out yourself?" Gabriel suggested, his frustration barely restrained.

"Told you," Walter snapped back as he settled into his La-Z-Boy. "Game's on." He dug in his pocket. "Here's the money for the tree."

"I'll pay for it." A curtain seemed to come down

over Gabriel's features. Silently, he held the door open for Olivia and his sons. The boys ran to the car and clambered into their seats in the back. When Gabriel started to get into the driver's seat, Olivia cleared her throat.

"You want me to open your door for you?" he asked, his tone biting.

"No," she replied, although she was thinking, *You were kinder as a boy.* But when she glanced at the twins in the backseat, she caught herself before she said something she'd regret. "I thought you might want to get some twine or rope to fasten the tree to the top of the car, and maybe an old blanket for padding."

"I'm one step ahead of you," he said, sliding behind the wheel as she got in the passenger side. "This car was actually home for three days right after the storm. Everything we could salvage was lashed to the roof. I still have the bungee cords in the back. As for padding, I'm beyond caring about the car's finish."

Justin, from his seat in the back, began to run through the songs from the pageant, while Jared snapped his fingers in rhythm—a pretty neat trick for a five-year-old. Olivia was glad they were happy about this outing, but she'd already delivered the recorder. Her errand was finished.

"Once we get to the center," she said, "I can walk across the street and I'll be home."

"I know where you live." There was a huskiness in Gabriel's voice that spoke to a certain Saturday night.

"I meant I don't have to help you pick out a tree. I only came over to give Jared the recorder. I didn't mean to get into the middle of family tree buying."

"You don't have to be. Just because Walter threw us together doesn't mean you have to stick to his script. Suit yourself."

What was wrong with this man's social skills? It wasn't as if she was fishing for a personal invitation. Put off by Gabriel's dismissal, Olivia looked out the car window to focus on residents who were busy decorating the exterior of their homes for the season.

"Look! There's Rudolph!" Justin exclaimed. "Can you see it, Jared?"

"Why did you even bother agreeing to get a tree now?" Olivia asked Gabriel under her breath.

"The boys were stoked about having their own Christmas tree this year." He kept his eyes on the road. "And you saw that pitiful artificial thing. Nothing good was going to come of that. Plus, any excuse to get out of the house."

Reminded of his situation, she softened. Could she say for sure she wouldn't be as put out and abrupt in his situation? "I'm sorry…about you and your dad."

"Don't be. Walter and I are never going to share a Kodak moment. But that's fine with me. He treats the boys okay, and that's all that matters."

"He actually seems to relish his role as grandfather," Olivia said, eager to steer the conversation away from potentially dangerous territory. "On the porch, he told me he hadn't put up a tree since your mother died. So maybe your return to Hennings is good for him."

"Let's just say he's not falling all over himself thanking me. Maybe, just maybe, I could better deal with the old curmudgeon if I knew why he seemed to think he had to be so tough on me. He's not this way with Daniel, you know."

She did know. And she knew why Walter had a hard time dealing with Gabriel. But she didn't think it was her story to tell. So why did she feel a twinge of guilt?

For the rest of the brief ride to the rec center, Gabriel stared through the windshield and tried to ignore Olivia's presence next to him. Although he was glad for an excuse to get out of Walter's house, he knew exactly what the old man was up to. He'd seized an opportunity to throw Olivia and Gabriel together. Like a family. Choosing a Christmas tree. How much more obvious could you get?

Well, Gabriel planned to get the tree, but he wasn't getting sucked into Walter's scheme.

"You can pull into my driveway." Olivia's voice intruded on his resolve. "Their parking lot's pretty much taken up with trees."

"I see Austin!" Justin exclaimed.

"Yes," Olivia replied, spying one of her students running around the rec center lot. "Ms. Van Dyke is volunteering at the sale. I bet she'd like it if you two boys kept Austin busy for a few minutes."

They were supposed to help pick out the tree, Gabriel thought, turning into Olivia's driveway, and not wanting to be left alone with her in the frosty air. With holiday carols being broadcast from outdoor speakers. And chestnuts roasting by an open fire... Damn, a volunteer on the tree lot actually had chestnuts roasting on an open fire. And another was manning an eggnog stand. Gabriel could use the eggnog to get through this greeting-card experience. A double shot of nog. Hold the egg.

"Hold my hands to cross the street," he said as he let the boys out of the car.

"Hold Ms. Marshall's hand, too," Justin countered.

"I'm not coming," Olivia replied.

"Why not? You told Grampa you'd help pick out a tree. That's a promise, isn't it?"

Gabriel couldn't stand the crestfallen look on his sons' faces. "It'll only take a couple minutes," he said to Olivia.

"If the boys want me to, okay." It looked as if she might deck him, given the opportunity.

"Hold Ms. Marshall's hand, too," Justin commanded once again.

"I only have two hands."

Jared solved that problem. With elfin glee, he put Justin's hand in Gabriel's, Gabriel's in Olivia's and Olivia's in his own. Then he beamed up at his dad, as if he was in on Walter's plot.

Gabriel had to admit that Olivia's hand in his felt warm...and somehow right.

No, he didn't have to admit it. To admit it would lead to a Saturday night sequel, and that wasn't going to happen. He walked across the street as quickly as traffic allowed.

"Olivia!" the woman volunteer called out. "Tell me you're here to relieve me. Austin's run out of what little patience he ever had. I thought Carl Obermeyer was to take the next shift, but he hasn't shown."

"Sorry. We're here to get Justin and Jared a tree."

"Oh, you must be their father." The woman held out a mittened hand to him, allowing him to drop Olivia's. "I'm Bonnie Van Dyke. Austin's mom." Her hand wasn't the perfect fit Olivia's had been.

"Gabriel Brant," he replied, pushing away rogue thoughts. As Justin and Jared tugged at his coat, he looked about the lot to get himself back on track. "The boys and I better start looking."

"Dad!" Justin said. "We wanna play with Austin."

"Oh, great. Here's Carl now," Bonnie said. "Finally, I can get Austin home and into a more controlled environment. I swear, I thought he might set off a domino effect with the trees. Austin, it's time to go home!"

When Justin and Jared looked disappointed, Bonnie turned to Gabriel. "Please, let me take your boys home for a couple of hours. Austin would love the company. You'd be doing me a favor." She pointed to a house three doors down from Olivia's, with a huge inflatable snow globe on the lawn. "I live just over there. And I have your address on the updated class roster. I'll have your boys home by five."

In not wanting them to go, he wasn't being an overprotective father. He was simply being a coward. If he didn't want to create a family holiday scene with Olivia and the boys, he sure didn't want to be left alone with her, either. Not with "Snuggle Up, My Silly Santa Sweetie" playing over the loudspeaker. Where had they come up with that sorry excuse for a song?

"We're gonna go home and play with you," Justin announced to Austin, as he ran up to them. The twins' unabashed eagerness decided the matter.

"Awright!" Austin replied. "I have tons of video games. Bet I can beat you both."

"Bet you can't!" Justin replied, all five-year-old swagger.

How could Gabriel refuse? He was a big boy. He'd survive picking out a tree with Olivia.

He made his sons look at him. "Remember, when you're in Austin's house, Ms. Van Dyke is the boss."

"Yessir!"

As quickly as that, his sons were gone, and he was left standing in a parking lot of listing evergreens with…

"Olivia, are you here for your tree?" Bonnie's replacement—Carl?—asked.

"N-no," she replied. She seemed disconcerted,

too. "We're here to get one for…Gabriel." She turned to him. "Now that the boys have gone, I really should go, too."

"Do you have your tree yet?" Carl pressed.

"Mmm, no."

"They're going fast. And it's just as easy to pick out two as one." What was this guy bucking for, salesman of the year? "Especially since you have a friend to help you drag it across the street."

"He has a point," Gabriel conceded. If she was looking for her own tree, she wouldn't be at his side, helping him pick out his.

"All right, I'll get my tree now," she said, as if she, too, just wanted to have this task over and done with. She headed off toward the tallest trees.

Gabriel headed down the row of the smallest ones. Walter's house wasn't much more than a cottage, and the two adults, at least, needed as much space to get away from each other as possible. Trying not to be swayed by the seductive odor of fir, not to think of this as a pleasure outing, Gabriel picked out the first tree that looked better to him than his father's artificial one. That was easy. When he went over to pay Carl, he noted that Olivia still hadn't moved far from where she'd started out. He chalked it up to a woman's natural browsing instinct. He might be here all afternoon. By the time he'd carried his tree across the street, strapped it to the top of his car and returned to help Olivia with hers, however, she was standing amid trees that completely dwarfed her.

"See anything you like?" he asked in an attempt to hurry her along.

"This one," she said, pointing to what had to be the tallest tree on the lot. "I already paid for it. I was just waiting for you to help me carry it."

"Where are you putting it? On your lawn? This thing belongs in Rockefeller Center."

"I'm putting it in my living room. I have ten-foot ceilings."

Why hadn't he remembered those beautiful old ceilings when he'd been in the house last? Oh, yeah, right. He'd been otherwise occupied.

He lifted one end and Olivia lifted the other and they carried the enormously heavy tree across the street and up onto her porch.

"Do you always get such a big tree?" he asked as she struggled to find her keys and open the front door.

"Always. The bigger the tree, the more powerful the aroma. And that many more branches for my ever-growing collection of ornaments my students have given me."

"And do you usually put it up alone? I mean, what if I hadn't come along?"

"More often than not, the custodian at the rec center helps me get it into the stand. Easy now." She guided him through the foyer and into the living room. "Right here next to the fireplace."

Right here next to the fireplace was where he'd wanted her. Where they'd almost…

"Merry Christmas! Don't forget the mistletoe! Burt wants a ginger cookie!"

"Burt needs to be patient," she said.

From his cage in the solarium, the parrot made a sound rather like a Bronx cheer.

"If you'll hold the tree," Olivia said to Gabriel, "I'll get the stand from the hall closet. I won't be a minute, but don't say anything you wouldn't want Burt to repeat to your sons and their classmates."

Now she tells me.

He held the tree upright and tried not to look at the sofa; tried to think of superficial conversation. A little chitchat to pass the time safely. He wasn't good at chitchat. "So, do you decorate your monster fir all by yourself?" he called after her, suddenly hoping she didn't do it by herself. Wasn't alone this time of year. A woman like Olivia, who gave so much to others, should have loved ones around her for the holidays.

She reappeared in the doorway, stand in hand. "My bunco club always holds its December game here. And everyone pitches in to decorate the tree. How it looks the next morning depends on how much schnapps we consumed the night before."

He actually felt a chuckle rise in his throat. "Are you sure Aunt Lydia would approve?"

"She would not." Olivia looked at him with a twinkle in her eye. "Aunt Lydia only drank sherry."

"Pour me a wee nip, Olivia!" the parrot ordered, in a voice Gabriel could still recognize as Lydia Marshall's.

"Ignore him," Olivia said. "He likes to act the bad boy."

"Baaad boy, baaad boy, watcha gonna *do!*"

"If you can manage to hold the tree a few inches off the floor," she said, ignoring the bird's lounge routine, "I'll slide the stand in place and attach it."

The only way to accomplish that was to grasp the tree trunk with both hands, which left Gabriel face deep in the fragrant boughs. What a stimulus to memory scent was. He found himself suddenly recalling the excitement, the magic of childhood Christmases, when anything seemed possible.

"You can let go now," Olivia said.

That was the problem. He had let go—of the magic—years ago. Post Katrina, he'd tried to create holiday cheer for his young sons, but though they seemed to get a kick out of his small efforts, he didn't feel the limitless possibilities in his bones.

"Oh, it's absolutely lovely!" Olivia exclaimed, standing now, looking at the tree, her face suffused with joy. "Maybe I won't decorate it this year. Maybe I'll leave it natural."

Natural. Like her. Naturally warm. Naturally generous. Naturally beautiful.

"I'd better get going," he said, the words sticking in his throat. If he stayed, he was certainly going to kiss her.

She caught him with her perceptive gaze. "We always seem to be trying to get away from each other," she said. "Why do you think that is?"

"Why do you?" He saw her glance at the sofa. "Maybe because we're not kids anymore. Maybe we've learned about consequences."

"Then why do you think we're still drawn to each other?"

He looked pointedly at the sofa himself. Sex. Sexual attraction was powerful enough to draw the most unlikely of couples together.

"Maybe each of us has something the other needs." She stood close enough to him that he could see flecks of gold in the soft brown of her eyes.

"*Wants,*" he corrected. "Maybe we each have something the other wants. There's a difference."

"Maybe they can be one and the same."

"Are you tempting me?"

"No! It wouldn't be—as we often say in kindergarten—appropriate."

"But it's appropriate to talk about it?"

"It's honest. And adult."

She had him there.

"Besides," she added, "Justin and Jared aren't going to be in my class forever."

"Wow! When you let down your teacher mask, you really let it down."

"Don't make fun of me. I took a big risk lowering that mask. I feel extremely vulnerable right now."

How could a woman be bold and vulnerable at the same time? Gabriel didn't know, but he found it a turn-on. "What are you saying?"

"That maybe we shouldn't deny the possibility of someday…"

"Oh, no. In case you hadn't noticed, guys come with on-off switches. There's no *maybe* switch." He had to hold himself back from reaching out for her. "I'm not staying in Hennings. You are. And with you, I really wouldn't want to start something I couldn't finish."

She seemed to retreat behind the mask. "I don't think you'll leave Hennings, but that's just a personal prediction."

"If I recall, your predictions were always wrong in the old days," he said, glad for a chance at a lighter direction. "Like the summer of '83, you predicted Madonna's debut album would be a flop and she'd never have any kind of career. Your fortune-teller's ball always needed a little Windex."

"Get the Windex, Olivia!" the parrot squawked. "My mirror's foggy!"

Unexpectedly, Gabriel found he didn't want to leave her. He wanted to stick around and, if not help decorate her tree, then at least fix a leaky faucet or plane a warped door or prepare her a meal. She made him want to take care of her.

Was he out of his ever-loving mind?

"I have to get our tree to Walter's and put it up so the boys can decorate it when Austin's mom brings them back," he said.

"Of course." There was disappointment in her eyes, but she held her chin high. "I'm glad you went for the real tree. Walter's artificial one was pretty pathetic."

"We agree on something, then."

Gabriel left her, and thought about nothing but wants and needs—and their tentative dance around the possibilities—driving the couple blocks back to 793 Chestnut.

After manhandling his tree through the front door, he set it down to await Walter's inevitable critique. Walter was still in the La-Z-Boy, but the TV had been turned off. The room seemed unnaturally silent.

"You didn't notice we had a guest?" Walter asked, nodding toward the chair that used to be Marjorie's. In it sat a woman Gabriel had to glance at twice to recognize.

Morgana was here in Hennings.

CHAPTER NINE

MORGANA STARR. At least that had been her stage name when Gabriel had last seen her. No matter if she'd changed it, she was still the mother of his sons. The woman he hadn't seen in four years.

"Surprise!" she said, shrugging coquettishly. Wearing a tight pink T-shirt with *Diva* spelled out on the front in rhinestones, Morgana was curled up, barefoot, in his mother's chair. Making herself at home.

Her appearance certainly was a surprise. Although he'd thought they'd have to get together at some point to iron out a legal custody arrangement, he hadn't had the extra money and so he hadn't sent her bus fare.

"I was telling your dad," she said, snuggling against the back of the chair as if she was settling in for a long, cozy chat, "how my girlfriend loaned me the money to come north. Especially after I showed her your letter and told her how you and I needed to work out a permanent solution for the boys. So where are they?"

The boys. Gabriel glanced at his watch. Bonnie Van Dyke had said she'd have Justin and Jared back by five. It was now four twenty-five. Thirty-five minutes to create a plan for handling a ticklish reunion. "At a friend's house."

Walter got up from his chair. "I'll make some coffee." For once, the old man made himself scarce without his usual acerbic commentary.

Gabriel leaned the Christmas tree against the wall, then sat on the sofa, which had been shoved in the corner to make room for the tree. Morgana watched him expectantly. He noticed now how her makeup almost, but not quite, concealed a black eye.

"Well, aren't you going to say anything?" she asked.

"Sorry. You caught me off guard. I guess I thought we'd get together sometime after the holidays."

"Me, too. But then I saw the postmark on your letter and I got to thinking about holiday TV specials and white Christmases. And my girlfriend had the extra cash, and she's a sucker for anything family...." Morgana brushed the side of her face tentatively. "And Max—he's my boss—told me to take time off until my eye wasn't Technicolor anymore. The milk of human kindness doesn't exactly gush through his veins, let me tell you."

Gabriel glanced at his watch again. "Morgana, I don't mean to be rude, but the boys are due back in thirty minutes. I think we need to dispense with the small talk and figure out how we're going to handle them seeing you again. They were only one when you left, so…"

"What have you told them?" She suddenly looked sad. "Am I dead?"

"No. Quite frankly, they were too young to ask any questions. Then Katrina struck, and they witnessed so many families in turmoil that after that our threesome didn't seem particularly unusual."

"They've never asked about me?"

"Justin has a couple times."

"And what did you tell him?"

"I told him his mom was sick and needed to go away to get better. I have to ask now—are you clean?"

"I am. Although I'm not going to lie to you. It hasn't been easy. But I wouldn't have come if I was still using. I'm at least that smart."

"I'm just thinking of the boys."

"Me, too." Her expression went from dead serious to little-girl curious, and Gabriel remembered how mercurial she'd been when he knew her. It was part of what had attracted him to her in the first place. "So that's all you told him? That I was sick?"

"I told both of them their mom—you—loved them so much you left them with me. Because you knew I'd always love and take care of them."

"That's sweet, Gabriel." Morgana hugged herself, as if she was cold. "But, then, you always were a sweet guy."

Oh, yeah. That's how he'd describe himself.

"You said Justin asked about me. How about Jared?"

"Jared hasn't spoken ever since the storm."

Morgana's eyes grew wide. She looked trapped, as if she wouldn't know what to do in such a situation.

"Don't worry. He's okay physically. It's just going to take more time for him to come around. To feel secure again. That's why I brought the boys back here. I figured Hennings would be sort of like comfort food." For the boys, maybe.

"Don't I know it already." Morgana giggled. "It looks like a set from some forties' movie. That one with Jimmy—or is it Jon?—Stewart. The one they always show at Christmas. Do you know this place still has a YWCA that rents rooms to women? That's where I'm staying."

That solved one problem. Gabriel tried hard not to let out a big sigh of relief.

"If you want coffee," Walter called from the kitchen, "you gotta come in here and get it."

Morgana uncurled from her seat. "Your dad's sweet," she said, making Gabriel realize the word for her was just a filler. "I could just eat him up," she added, padding out to the kitchen. As if Walter's house was a form of comfort food and she was settling in for a big meal.

Gabriel followed and noted Morgana's tight, low-slung jeans. They didn't leave much to the imagination, for sure. She'd always exhibited such a split personality—innocent little girl one minute, provocative siren the next. And you could never tell which one was about to surface on any given occasion. How long was she planning to stay in Hennings, anyway, and while she did, how the hell was Gabriel going to explain her?

Olivia immediately came to mind. As if he somehow owed her an explanation.

In the kitchen, he faced another puzzle. Walter. The old man definitely was behaving oddly. With a circumspection Gabriel wouldn't have thought possible. As Morgana sat at the table and chatted cheerily about everything and nothing, his father seemed to listen to her. Without comment, he drank his coffee, even nodded occasionally, with a gravity and deference he usually only bestowed upon FOX News. Standing at the sink, apart from the pair, Gabriel couldn't figure out if Morgana had won Walter over, and if his dad had now turned his matchmaking attentions away from Olivia. A bird in the hand…

A draft of cold air scuttled across the floor as the front door opened and Justin and Jared dashed through the house into the kitchen. They came to an abrupt halt when they saw Morgana.

Gabriel realized the adults still hadn't come to any agreement on how to reintroduce the boys to their mother.

The twins sidled close to him. In a stage whisper, Justin asked, "Who's she?"

"I'm…Morgana," she said, standing up. Actually, she unwound herself, catlike, from the chair she'd been sitting in. "I'm your..." Her gaze darted to Gabriel. "I'm your daddy's friend from a long time ago, and I'm in town for a visit."

Walter looked visibly relieved, and Gabriel wondered why, after four years away, a woman might travel hundreds of miles to see her sons and not reveal herself to them as their mother. Was she suddenly frightened? Ashamed? What was really going on here?

"I like your T-shirt," Justin said. "It's sparkly."

Morgana puffed out her considerable chest to look down at the rhinestone lettering. "It sure is," she said, sounding less like a pro in the exotic dance business and more like a proud kid. "Sparkly things make me happy."

"They make Ms. Marshall's parrot happy, too," Justin replied. "That's why you have to keep his mirror clean."

"Who's Ms. Marshall?"

"Our teacher. She's pretty."

Morgana pretended to look hurt. "Am I pretty?"

"Yes'm," Justin replied shyly.

"Well, I'd like to meet your teacher. Then you could have two pretty girls in your life."

Great. Just how involved was Morgana—as a "friend"—planning to get?

IT WAS TEN O'CLOCK and Gabriel had to be up for his diner shift tomorrow at five in the morning. He wished he was in bed, instead of walking Morgana back to her room at the Y. She'd stayed for supper and the decorating of the tree, as well as the boys' baths and story time. The evening had been painfully surreal. Gabriel had found it difficult to consider Morgana as one of the adults, especially when she'd curled up on Jared's bed as Gabriel had read the twins *Cowardly Clyde,* a book Olivia had sent home from the classroom. With her arms wrapped tightly around a pillow and her eyes saucer-wide during the story, Morgana had seemed roughly the same age as the twins. Gabriel wondered, not for the first time, what it really was she sought to gain from this trip.

And now, without the boys and Walter around, he could ask.

"I'm disappointed there's no snow," Morgana said, twirling around on the empty sidewalk, her face tilted over one shoulder to catch her reflection in the hardware-store window. "Don't you think it would be cool to have a snowball fight with the boys?"

"Morgana, why didn't you tell them you were their mother?"

She stopped twirling. Her shoulders slumped. "I chickened out. It's been four years, and if you only knew, I haven't had much practice being motherly. I don't want to hurt them."

"Then what do you want from us?"

"I'm...not sure." She stopped under a streetlight

that was trimmed with a snowflake banner. Gazing up at him, she was the little girl again. Petite, insecure and looking for someone to take care of her. The woman who'd once admitted to him that Morgana Starr was her stage name. She'd been born Cheryl Watson. Cheryl, she'd said, was painfully shy, but Morgana could be sexy and even reckless.

"Before I got your letter," she said, "I used to think about the boys. A lot. But I never worried, because I knew they were in good hands. Then, when your letter arrived, and you asked to have full custody, I began to wonder if I couldn't be a mother again, after all. Now that I'm clean."

Gabriel had thought the bottom had fallen out of his life with Katrina, but that devastation was nothing compared to the cold emptiness he now felt in the pit of his stomach. "Are you saying you'd fight me for custody?"

"Why would we have to fight? Why can't things go on as before? Maybe with me seeing them a little bit more."

The cold began to seep into his marrow. "What do you mean by 'a little bit more?'"

They stepped aside for a group of revelers coming out of Harry's Sasquatch Tavern. One of the men gave Morgana the visual once-over before moving on.

"Well, of course, the boys would stay in Hennings to go to school," she said, not indifferent to the appraisal. "But on vacations—some vacations—maybe they could come stay with me."

"You…work. What kind of child care could you arrange?"

"Gee, I hadn't thought of that. I don't think Max would let them come to the club."

"Neither would I."

"No. I guess it's not the *proper* environment for five-year-olds." She looked genuinely disappointed. "And my boyfriend…" She fingered the edges of her blackened eye. "My soon-to-be ex-boyfriend, maybe, doesn't like kids."

Gabriel bit back a curse. "The twins should stay here."

"Then, I could visit you guys when I get time off? I already told the boys I was an old friend of yours. Maybe they could call me Auntie."

"Morgana, stop. Justin and Jared aren't a couple of kittens. You don't play with them, play with their emotions, and then foist them off on someone else until you have a little more time to play with them again. It doesn't work that way. As their mother, you're either a part of their lives—a responsible, adult part—or you give me the legal right to raise them."

"You're right. Of course. I guess that's why I didn't tell them I was their mother. I need to see if I'm up to all this." Deflated, she sat down on a bench in front of the florist's and hugged herself. "Geez, do you think it could get any colder?"

After four years, she wanted to experiment? How could she do this to all of them? Gabriel tamped down his rising anger by trying to think about what it must have cost her to give the boys up in the first place. By focusing on what it would cost him to give them up—for any length of time—now.

"How long do you think it'll take you to decide?" he asked, standing in front of her and stamping his feet to keep warm.

"I took two weeks off, but with travel time I'd probably have to head back to Oklahoma next Monday."

A week. She was sticking around a week. But she might as well have said a year. That's how long it seemed.

"You don't look happy," she said, glancing up, sweetly solicitous.

He wasn't happy.

When he didn't respond, she hopped up, linked her arm with his and began to walk, leaning softly into him. "I know you just got here yourself, and you're still settling in. But you don't have to entertain me. I grew up in a town like this. Staying here will be like coming home. Just without my own family screaming at me. Plus, I'll be a big help with the boys—you just wait and see."

Sure. Why did he feel that now, instead of having two kids to watch over, he was going to have three?

She squeezed his arm and said, "Besides, Walter's house could use a woman's touch."

Oh, Walter was going to love this.

She stopped and looked back at the florist's. "You know, that wreath on the door was awfully pretty. It sure would brighten up my room at the Y. And being a flower shop, they could easily replace it."

He grasped her wrist.

"Just kidding." She smiled, flashing her dimples. "As a mom, from now on I'm going to act real mature. But I've gotta say you've kinda turned into an old party poop, Gabriel."

They walked the rest of the way up Main Street to the Y in a one-sided silence. Gabriel didn't speak, and Morgana chattered nonstop, pointing out Christmas decorations and lights with all the enthusiasm of a child.

They'd talked about the boys. They'd even touched upon the topic of Walter. What made Gabriel most uneasy was the fact that he didn't know where he fit into Morgana's plans.

With all that had already gone on today, he sure didn't have the energy to open that can of worms.

MONDAY AFTERNOON at dismissal, Olivia stood under the school portico with her class, waiting for parents and guardians to pick up her students.

Justin pointed. "There's Grampa with Morgana."

She saw Walter approaching with a woman at his side. There was an unaccustomed spring to the man's step, and as the pair neared, Olivia could guess why. The woman—much, much younger than Walter—was extremely pretty. Pretty in the way of the Barbie doll Olivia had bought with her allowance money as a young girl and had hidden under her bed because Aunt Lydia thought her an "unrealistic role model for a strong young woman." While most of the other women braving the cold— Olivia included—were dressed in layers of warm clothing that made them look like pot stickers, this woman was dressed in skintight jeans, a cropped pink leather jacket with pink fur trim, pink ugg boots and a blindingly white knit cap and mittens. Her smile, when she spied Justin and Jared, was just as blindingly white.

"There are my favorite boys!" she called, as she skipped the rest of the way to envelop the twins in an exuberant double hug. The boys didn't seem totally comfortable in the embrace.

"I'm Olivia Marshall," Olivia said, extending her hand. "Justin and Jared's teacher."

"She's the one with the parrot," Justin stated.

"Morgana Starr." As the woman shook hands, she eyed Olivia thoughtfully. "The boys talk about you a lot. You must be good at what you do." There was a wistful quality to the way she spoke.

"Thank you."

"And you sure are pretty. Just like he said."

"T-thank you." Who was *he?*

Walter came up alongside, puffing audibly. "Morgana's in town for a while. She wants to be as much a part of the boys' routine as possible."

At first Olivia didn't get the connection, but then she looked more closely at the woman's face. And saw Justin and Jared reflected there. "Oh! You must be—"

"A friend of Gabriel's." Walter cut in emphatically. "She's staying *at the Y.* Got anything in the classroom she can help with?" It almost seemed as if he was trying to off-load her.

"Well…" Olivia was puzzled at Walter's qualifying remarks, then remembered how Gabriel had failed to list a mother on the boys' registration. Did the twins know who she was? "We can always use volunteers."

"I don't know," Morgana replied. "Schools and hospitals always give me the creeps. No offense."

"None taken." But then Olivia didn't really see how the woman could be involved in any meaningful way. At least not during the boys' school day. With Gabriel at work, Walter would just have to entertain her.

Justin tugged on her sleeve. "What about the pageant?"

"The pageant, of course!" Morgana exclaimed. "What a good idea, Jared."

Olivia glanced at the boys to see their response to Morgana's gaffe with the twins' names. Jared looked at the ground, while Justin rolled his eyes. "It's a children's program."

"Oh, they've told me all about it. It sounds like fun. Don't you have anything adults can do?"

"We certainly could use help with painting scenery or making costumes."

"Costumes! I make all my own costumes, and I've been told I'm very creative."

"Are you an actress?" Judging by the panicked look on Walter's face, Olivia suspected she'd delved too deeply.

"I am in the entertainment industry, yes," Morgana replied. "So, when would you need me?"

"We're working tonight at the rec center. We have two more weeks until the performance, and the dress rehearsal's this coming Saturday. Unfortunately, we left the hardest costumes until last. You wouldn't have any ideas for snowflakes, would you?"

"Honey, I'm a whiz with anything that sparkles."

"I have to warn you we'll probably work late."

"Oh, you don't have to worry about me. I'm a night owl." She turned a megawatt smile on Walter. "If you'll get me to this rec center, I'm sure Gabriel can pick me up after his shift. You know, strange streets and all, and me without a car. I may stay up late, but I'm sort of afraid of the dark."

Jared poked Justin in the side.

Olivia wasn't sure quite how she felt about this turn of events, but she wasn't—absolutely wasn't—going to get herself stuck in the middle of this new Brant family dynamic. Perhaps Morgana's arrival in town had solved Olivia's personal dilemma.

"Who wants pie?" Morgana asked the boys.

"We do!" Justin replied.

"Then let's go see your daddy at the diner. If I remember, he made the best pecan pie in the whole world."

"He still does," Justin declared with unabashed pride.

"Well, lead the way." Morgana winked at Olivia. "Three handsome escorts. How lucky can a woman get?"

Lucky. Very, very lucky, Olivia thought, as Justin and Jared slipped their hands into their mother's.

CHAPTER TEN

TWO WEEKS INTO HIS job and Gabriel was hoping Marmaduke wouldn't fire him.

After Morgana, Walter and the kids had come into the diner for pie and ice cream, Gabriel had lost his focus. Who wouldn't have, when Morgana declared she'd signed on as a volunteer in Olivia's pageant? Subsequently, Gabriel scorched the dirty rice he'd planned for that night's special étouffée. He'd nearly sliced off the tip of his finger, chopping scallions. And then he'd yelled at Heather, the new waitress, making her cry and threaten to quit before the shift was over. As soon as Gabriel had prepared the last order, even while customers were still eating in the dining room, Marmaduke had pushed him out of the kitchen, telling him to go home, get some sleep and get his head on straight.

Gabriel wished it was that easy.

Instead, he was heading to the rec center, as he'd promised, to walk Morgana back to her room after her volunteer stint. He wasn't cut out for the Sir Galahad role, and he hoped the work session was over and done with, because he didn't feel like hanging around the center, either. Didn't feel like running into Olivia.

Too bad for him.

The center was ablaze with lights and abuzz with activity, with Morgana right in the thick of it all.

"I suppose I should thank you."

Gabriel turned to see Olivia standing beside him. "Why?" When he couldn't take back the bite in his response, he wondered if he'd become a grumpy old man at thirty-four. Damn. Was he turning into Walter?

Olivia didn't seem to let his foul mood affect her upbeat one. Or else she hid her emotions well. She smiled and nodded in the direction of Morgana, who was swathed in yards of some gauzy silver material and playfully directing several men in the painting of enormous snowflake cutouts.

"After helping their wives carry in supplies," Olivia explained, "quite a few husbands decided to stay. We can always use the extra hands."

"Morgana has that effect," he replied drily. "Any problems with the women?"

"Not at all. There's something very likable about Morgana. Something childlike despite her…physical attributes."

"Is there a point to this conversation?" He needed to get home.

"Yes." Olivia drew him even farther from the volunteer groups. "Please don't think I'm prying into your affairs, but…as Justin and Jared's teacher

I need to know a few basics. So that I don't step on a land mine when I'm talking to the boys."

"What do you need to know?"

"Walter introduced Morgana as a *friend*. Do the twins not know she's their mother?"

"You don't beat around the bush, do you? Who told you?"

"Nobody. But you only have to look at their faces to see the connection."

When he didn't answer, she rested her hand on his arm. He felt her touch as an accusation and he recoiled.

"Gabriel," she said softly, "my intention isn't to interfere. I want to make sure I go along with whatever plan you've made to handle the situation."

"I'm afraid we don't have a plan. We're all kind of flying by the seat of our pants."

She looked directly at him, and he didn't think he could bear the sympathy he read in her eyes.

"The boys don't know," he said. "At the last minute Morgana couldn't bring herself to tell them. She wants some time to figure out what to do."

"With the boys."

"With…everything."

For the briefest of moments, he thought he saw disappointment in her features. "It's just that the twins are so vulnerable," she said. "Especially Jared. I don't want to do or say anything to upset them. My job is to create a safe learning environment. Within the classroom."

She said the last with emphasis, and he could tell she was struggling to find a neutral and professional tone.

"Olivia." Her name on his tongue felt intimate. And disconcerting. "You've been good for my kids. They've made progress with you. I'd hoped…" He cleared his throat, veering away from what it was he might have hoped for on a gut level. "That's why I didn't want them split up. Why I wanted them to stay in your class."

"Thank you," she replied softly, glancing at Morgana, who had her head thrown back in a laugh.

"She hasn't been in the picture for a very long time," he said. "We—"

"Gabriel, honey!" Morgana had spotted him. "Come see the snowflake costumes we're making."

"I have to get up early tomorrow," he told Olivia, and then he headed toward Morgana. Although he wanted to stay and explain to Olivia that there was nothing between him and his ex-girlfriend now. Oh, yeah. Nothing, if you didn't count two kids. And several major unresolved issues. But why should he explain? There was nothing between him and Olivia, either.

Olivia watched Gabriel walk away, and wondered why she felt so upset. He'd given her the information she needed, in order to interact with Justin and Jared. As their teacher. He didn't owe her anything more than that. So why did she wish he did?

She busied herself, picking up and locking away as many of the supplies as would fit in the center's cabinets. When she finally took a look around the room, Gabriel and Morgana were gone.

"Gabriel's girlfriend is a hoot," Lynn said, coming up and handing Olivia the costume, prop and scenery list with completed items crossed off.

"Why do you assume she's Gabriel's girlfriend?"

"Well, one, he came to walk her home. And did you see the way she lit up when she saw him?"

"Oh, like the way she lit up when she saw each and every man who walked into the room?"

Lynn laughed. "So she's a natural flirt. She's harmless. Besides," she added, glancing at her husband, "because of her, I might get lucky tonight. Cary's engine is already warmed up."

"You're so bad."

"No, I'm a realist."

That's what Olivia needed to be. A realist. Not some damsel in a fairy tale, mooning over Mr. Tall, Dark and Distant.

"Did I tell you Will's still talking about the superintendent's ball?" Will was Lynn's cousin and he'd recently been Olivia's blind date for the annual school district event. She'd gone with another of Lynn's cousins the year before. "He had a great time."

Lynn took the stack of folded costumes from Olivia's arms. Funny, but she didn't remember either picking up the costumes or folding them.

"Olivia? Your response should be either, 'So did I, and I'd like to see him again' or 'Sorry, but he's just not my type.'"

"I had a great time, too, but…sorry, he's just not my type."

"And your type would be…? Come on, help me out a little here. I'm running out of cousins."

"I don't know." But Olivia did. "I guess I'll know when I meet him." And she had met him.

The women finished cleaning up, then turned out the lights and parted on the rec center's front steps. Olivia pulled her hat down over her ears and hugged her coat closely to her chest to ward off the bitter cold as she ran across the street to her house. The night was clear, and before climbing the porch steps she looked up at the moon, hoping to see a ring around it. Hoping for a sign of snow. Cold, without snow, was no fun at all. Cold, without snow, wasn't the least bit like Christmas.

"Let it snow! Let it snow! Let it snow!" she sang out, then stopped herself, remembering Morgana taking delighted control of the costumes for that very pageant number.

At the thought of the beautiful and flirtatious woman, Olivia felt surprisingly jealous. And she didn't like the feeling. Aunt Lydia would say it was unbecoming. Besides, Morgana had been a wonderful help. If she'd been just another new volunteer, if Gabriel hadn't come to pick her up, Olivia probably would have invited her home for a glass of wine and a single girls' chat. But Gabriel *had* come for Morgana....

Olivia turned her key in the lock and immediately was soothed by the scent of evergreen.

"Here comes Santa Claus! Here comes Santa Claus—right down Santa Claus Lane!" Burt's favorite season was Christmas, and his favorite Christmas voice was Gene Autry's, which he did to pure retro perfection.

Olivia laughed aloud at his greeting and felt better. Entering the living room and switching on the lights of her Christmas tree, she felt still more cheerful. She had a lot to look forward to. Friday's bunco party, when she'd finish decorating the tree. Saturday's dress rehearsal for the pageant. Then Sunday's Christmas caroling. Maybe she should do Aunt Lydia proud, be a big girl and invite Morgana to the party.

Her doorbell rang. Probably it was Lynn wanting one last word on pageant changes before tumbling into bed with preheated Cary.

Not Lynn, but Gabriel stood on her front porch. Alone. And looking way too sexy for his own good.

And hers.

Gabriel took a deep breath as Olivia opened the door. He shouldn't have come, but he couldn't stop himself. In fact, he'd been headed toward this moment ever since Morgana had walked into the diner earlier that afternoon and let him know her path was going to cross Olivia's. And ever since the rec center, when Olivia had quietly accepted his in-adequate explanation.

He needed to explain.

No, if he was honest, he needed Olivia.

And here she stood, backlit by the lights on her tree, looking like a Christmas angel.

"May I come in?" If she said no, that she was busy or it was too late, he'd go away. And stay away.

"Of course." She held the door open wider, as if she knew full well what he was really asking.

He stepped into the foyer and shrugged out of his jacket. She took it from him and hung it on a coat stand in the corner.

"Come into the living room," she said. "I'll start a fire."

He didn't need a fire. He was warm already. Very warm. Still, he followed her into the room, which was lit only by the magical glow of Christmas tree lights.

"I…I didn't do a very good job," he began as she lit the kindling, "of explaining Morgana."

If he expected her to reply, "No need," she surprised him. She didn't speak, but knelt before the fireplace and blew gently on the glowing embers. And waited.

"We're not married." He might as well cut to the chase. "Never were. In fact, when we split and I left to start my restaurant in New Orleans, I didn't know she was pregnant. She might not have known, either. She's never said." Communication hadn't ever been their strong suit.

With a poker, Olivia nudged the growing fire, and then replaced the screen. She sat on the hearth rug, regarding him intently. He sat opposite and tried to concentrate on his story. Tried not to get sidetracked by how beautiful she looked in the firelight. Her dark hair falling softly over her shoulders, her eyes sparkling, her skin rosy and her mouth deliciously inviting.

"Then, obviously, Morgana came back into your life at some point," she said. "When?"

"When the boys were one. She brought them to me in New Orleans."

"You hadn't seen her in all that time?"

"No. And I didn't know about the boys."

"Did you try to make a go of it, then?"

He shook his head. "By then, she was hooked on cocaine. She needed me to take Justin and Jared so she could straighten out her life."

"Oh!" Olivia's response came with a quick intake of breath, as if she now realized how different their worlds had been. Were.

"She did the right thing," he said, suddenly feeling defensive. "She's clean now. No small feat."

Olivia's eyes grew misty. "I'm not passing judgment. I was just thinking how hard it must have been for her. To give up her babies. And how hard for you—to become an instant father."

He was taken aback. No one else had ever acknowledged how difficult it had been for him to go from being a bachelor to a man entrusted with the

care of two young children in the space of a minute.
Not just any children, either. His sons. He'd been
expected to feel an immediate bond, and yet, he was
ashamed to admit, he hadn't. It had taken months
and months of tying shoes and wiping noses and
reading bedtime stories to build the relationship.
And then, ironically, it had turned out that the
demon Hurricane Katrina had unleashed its fury
and cemented his love of his boys. Had shown him
how easily he could have lost what had become
dearest to him.

"Are you okay?" Olivia reached over and squeezed
his hands. Only as he felt the warmth of her touch did
he realize he'd grown cold despite the fire that was
crackling loudly not three feet away.

"Yeah. I'm okay."

"So she came back because she's off the drugs?"

"I don't really know why she came back now. The
fact that one of my letters finally reached her, maybe.
I don't know if she was trying to find me while I was
trying to find her. To get custody of the boys."

"She must be scared." The look in Olivia's eyes
was one of genuine concern. "Of losing her sons.
Yet, if she wants to stay in the picture, she must
wonder if the boys will accept her. If she can stay
clean for them. She must wonder…about you."

"That's what I had to tell you. I don't know what
she's thinking. About me. But I don't have any
feelings for her. Except that I'm grateful she did
what was best for our kids."

"Why are you telling me this?" The room, lit only by the fire and Christmas lights, seemed to grow smaller, to close around the two of them intimately.

"I think you know." He stood up, drawing her with him. He was prepared to make his admission—that she meant enough for him to be forthright—and then leave.

"I do know, and I'm glad." She leaned forward, brushing his lips with her own.

Need and want welled up in him, as it had on his first night in this room. But he pulled away from her. "I wanted to be honest with you. About my past. I've been honest with you about my future, too. I'm not staying in Hennings."

"Quite frankly," she replied, her voice husky with yearning, "I'm interested in the present."

Still he held back. "Why me?"

"I don't have an answer. Maybe because you were my friend first. Or because you're my opposite, and you're exciting. Then again, perhaps with some relationships we don't get to choose in any logical way."

"Getting involved with me in any way other than as my kids' teacher could screw up everything you've achieved for yourself in this town."

"Excuse me?"

"You have roots here, but Hennings is just a temporary stop for me. I have baggage. A lot of baggage."

"You don't think I have baggage?" There were tears in her eyes.

"If you do, you hide it really well. Whereas my life's a mess, you're totally in control of yours, with energy left over to spread good works all over town. My father called you the closest thing Hennings had to Mother Teresa."

"Do you know how that hurts me?" Olivia shook her head as if to clear the tears, then began to pace, her tone of voice and movements obviously disturbing the parrot in the adjoining solarium. He began to squawk and rustle about in his cage.

"It was a compliment, I'm sure."

"It totally negates the fact I'm a woman with a woman's wants and needs."

"Maybe people who don't know you personally only see the restrained professional."

"I'm a kindergarten teacher, for God's sake!" she nearly shouted. "Ninety percent of my life requires restraint."

"So you think maybe you'll go wild behind the scenes the other ten percent, with some guy who's just passing through? Is that the real you—or are you just having a game of pretend?"

"I think you'd better leave."

"So do I." He walked out of the living room and into the hallway.

He hadn't even gotten to the coatrack when a shoe sailed by his head, hit the front door, then clattered to the floor. "Maybe, just maybe, I'm tired of being Hennings's prissy patron saint!" Olivia yelled.

When he turned, she was standing in the archway between the hall and living room, hands on her hips, her eyes blazing. She didn't look like a kindergarten teacher with self-control to spare. But she looked a lot like the girl he knew from his childhood. The one who swung for the fences. Who never backed down from a challenge. Someone who wore her feelings on her sleeve, for better or worse.

He laughed, a deep laugh that came from a forgotten place inside him; that long unaccustomed reflex, a powerful erotic jolt. Crossing the hall, he drew her to him and kissed her hungrily.

As she lost herself in his kiss, Olivia knew, without question, that this was what she wanted. Wanted beyond all the reasons she could tick off why it could go wrong. She'd been hiding her wants behind that list of "shoulds," coasting on automatic pilot for so long. Gabriel, with his raw energy, made her feel truly alive.

She wouldn't think about him leaving town.

Instead, she gloried in touching him. In feeling his response. She would have this moment, ignoring both past and future. Pulling away from his kiss, she took his hand and led him to the stairs. If she was going to steal this moment, she was going to steal it on four-hundred-count sheets.

He stopped her at the bottom of the stairs. "I don't have protection."

"I do."

His eyes grew wide. "You're full of surprises."

"Oh, I'm even capable of surprising myself," she replied with a laugh before dashing up the stairs. Gabriel followed in hot pursuit.

On the landing they came together, breathlessly, their embrace as much release as passion. They were both grinning, as if this had become a dare.

"This is my bedroom," she whispered, pulling him into the front room stealthily, as if she'd sneaked him into the house and was now hiding him from her aunt.

He closed the door behind them as if he, too, felt the adventure in what they were doing, and then he kissed her on their way to the four-poster bed, his kisses rough and possessive. He tumbled her onto the soft duvet. Knelt above her. Suddenly serious, he undressed her with slow, accomplished movements. Watched her with eyes so blue and penetrating she felt as if they were caressing her.

When they were both naked in their private world under the antique lace canopy, he took her. And she took him.

CHAPTER ELEVEN

"I HAVE TO GO." Gabriel's voice came to Olivia from far away.

She felt the whisper of his kiss on an eyelid and stretched luxuriously, still half-asleep. But when she reached for him, he wasn't in bed. Frowning and opening her eyes, she saw him silhouetted against the windows and the streetlight beyond. He was putting on his clothes. Slowly. As if he didn't want to leave. It was dark outside, and the sensation of intimacy and seclusion still shrouded the room.

"I have to be at the diner in forty-five minutes," he said quietly. "To get ready for the breakfast shift. But first I have to check on the boys, before Walter gets them up and off to school. They'll be asleep and they won't even know I've been and gone, but I want to check on them anyway."

"Of course," she replied, rising. Wanting him with a new boldness she didn't know she possessed. "Do you have time for a cup of coffee?"

"No, thanks. Do you?" He nodded toward her bedside clock. It was four-fifteen.

On a school morning.

Her alarm was automatically set to go off in a little over an hour, and she'd caught maybe twenty minutes of sleep altogether. Not that she was complaining. She couldn't remember the last time she'd felt this good. Rested and energized at the same time. Satisfied.

"Didn't think so," he said, and Olivia caught a glimpse of a grin in the glow from the streetlight.

Throwing on a robe, she followed him downstairs and watched him shrug into his jacket. "Olivia," he said, his voice tentative.

"Shh!" She placed her fingers on his lips. She didn't want to hear again that he couldn't promise her a relationship. Didn't want to hear that he'd be leaving Hennings with the first good offer. That he'd enjoyed their single night of reckless passion, but that was all it could ever be. She wanted the moment to remain whole. Untarnished.

When he opened the door and then stepped out on the porch, she leaned against the jamb, heedless of the bitter cold. Despite her declarations of independence the night before, she didn't want him to leave. Halfway down the steps, he turned, then bounded back to her. Took her in his arms and kissed her as if he, too, was having trouble letting go. He left her breathless, but leave her he did, trotting down Winterberry Street toward Chestnut.

When her bare feet began to tingle from the cold, she shook herself back to reality. Turning to enter the house, she saw Adrienne Quincy, the mother of Robert, the most troublesome child in her classroom, walking the family's yellow lab. At least, she had been walking the dog. Now, she stood in the middle of the sidewalk, watching Gabriel's retreating form. When she looked at Olivia, she was smiling.

It wasn't a pleased-to-run-into-you-at-this-hour smile, either.

That smile brought back all the big reasons Olivia shouldn't have gotten involved with Gabriel. Giving in to the attraction, even for the short term, would mean keeping the relationship low-key— secret, even—until the end of the school year. And Olivia wasn't a secretive person.

And at the end of the school year, then what? What if Gabriel found a better job elsewhere? Uprooting the twins from their grandfather, their new home and their school would be wrenching enough. How much more difficult would it be, if they began to see Olivia as a mother figure, only to have that hope squashed?

Olivia found herself right back in the land of the *shoulds,* all over again.

GABRIEL WASN'T SURPRISED to find the light on in Walter's kitchen, but he *was* surprised to find the old man sitting at the table, coffee cup in hand, a game of solitaire spread out in front of him.

"Couldn't sleep?" Gabriel asked, helping himself to coffee.

"No. I was waiting for you. Where've you been all night?"

"Out." He didn't have the time or inclination for a grilling. As if he were a rebellious teenager. "I think I'm entitled to an occasional break."

"Don't be a smart-ass. And keep your voice down. The kids need their sleep."

"Look, I have to get to work."

"If you've taken up again with Morgana—"

"I haven't. Not that it's any of your business."

"None of my business?" Walter rose from his seat. "I goddamn well think it's my business," he hissed, trying to keep his voice down, "when I'm home babysitting two innocent little boys while their father's out tomcattin'."

Gabriel wanted to deny the accusation, but what exactly had he been up to?

"Where were you?" Walter repeated.

"This isn't working." Gabriel drained his cup of coffee. "Today I'll talk to Marmaduke about moving into one of his rentals." Although how he'd afford it, he didn't know. He couldn't even barter his services, because he needed his paychecks to whittle down his credit card debt. But he couldn't continue to live under his father's constant disapproving scrutiny. "The waitresses have offered to help me find child care—"

"No!" The old man's eyes grew wide. Almost fearful. "My grandsons don't need to be moved again."

"But you don't want the responsibility of watching them."

"I didn't say that." Walter actually seemed to back down. "What else have I got to do?"

Monitor my every move, Gabriel thought bitterly. "We need to hash this out," he said. "But later. Right now, I'm late for work."

Leaving Walter to stew in his own juices, he headed upstairs to look in on his sons. Pausing at the foot of their beds, gazing down on their sweet, trusting faces, he resolved, not for the first time, to do right by them. He quickly changed into clean clothes, then left the house by the front door.

All the anger that had been eased away by his stolen night with Olivia was back.

WHEN SHE ARRIVED at school, she found a note from Kelly in her mailbox. The clerk had already scheduled a parent-teacher conference for her after school today. With Adrienne Quincy.

"When did she call?" Olivia asked Kelly.

"It must have been at the crack of dawn," she replied. "There was a message to phone her back already on my machine when I got here this morning."

"Did she say what she wants to talk about?"

Kelly rolled her eyes. Only three and a half months into his school career, five-year-old Robert was recognized by the entire staff as a handful, and his mother was known to be extremely "involved" in her son's education. "Your guess is as good as mine."

Better than yours, Olivia thought ruefully as she made her way to her classroom, remembering Adrienne Quincy's expression as she'd witnessed Gabriel's departure.

That didn't stop Olivia from trying to modify Robert's behavior during the day. While most of his classmates had accepted Jared, Robert had seemed to make it his mission to make Jared speak or else make his life miserable. She'd separated the two as much as was possible, but Robert was sneaky. When the kids got to make choices, such as lining up for lunch or playing at recess, Robert always managed to wind up next to Jared. Although the encounters didn't escalate to physical fighting, they usually ended in squabbling and sometimes tears.

Near the end of the day, when she had refereed and counseled both boys till she was almost out of patience, she kept Jared behind while the rest of the class went to the library for story time and book exchange. She hated to have him miss out on any part of the school day, but there simply was no other time to talk to him one-on-one.

Jared seemed pleased to have her all to himself as she settled them both at one of the tables.

"Jared," she began, not quite certain how she was going to explain an adult concept to this young child, "many times we can't control what happens to us. Nobody could control a storm as big as Katrina, could they?"

Jared solemnly shook his head.

"But your dad had a choice after the storm. He could stay in New Orleans or he could bring you here to Hennings. And he chose Hennings."

A cloud seemed to lift from Jared's features.

"Do you like it in Hennings?"

He nodded.

"Do you like it in my classroom?"

He nodded vigorously.

"Well, in my classroom there are still some things you don't have any control over, and some things you do."

He seemed to think about it.

"Can you give me an example of what you just have to accept and do?"

With a twinkle in his eye, he pointed to the blackboard, where they'd been working their way through the alphabet. Today she'd introduced the letter T, with pictures cut from magazines of things with that letter in their name.

"Exactly. I expect you to learn in my classroom. Now, can you give me an example of a choice you can make?"

She expected him to point to the puzzle box or the BRIO town or the bookshelf, but instead he looked down at the table.

"Jared," she said gently, "please, look at me."

He did.

"You can choose how you have others treat you. I'm not saying you have to talk just to stop Robert's teasing. Although I know you can talk, and someday you're going to find something you think is important enough to say. Am I right?"

Slowly, very slowly, he nodded.

"I'm saying you have to do something even strong men find difficult. You have to ignore Robert, when he's not being the kind of friend you want. That way, even if you don't say a word, you send him a clear message. Do you think you can do that?"

He shrugged his small shoulders.

"Will you try? For me?"

He looked at her, adoration in his eyes, and nodded.

When she exhaled, she realized she'd been holding her breath. Realized she felt toward this child not just a teacher's commitment, but something much closer to a mother's protective instinct.

GABRIEL WAS GLAD TO SEE Justin and Jared bound into the diner after school, even if they did have Walter and Morgana in tow. Except for his day off and the couple of times during the weekly rotation when he didn't have the supper shift, he didn't get to see his sons much, and he looked forward to this new habit they'd developed of dropping in for a snack midafternoon, when he could take his break. It gave them a chance to talk about their day. To provide some fairly neutral territory for Walter and himself. Now, with Morgana in the mix, he was back to walking on eggshells even here.

As usual, the boys had a sheaf of drawings.

"So what happened in school today, guys?" he asked, dishing out bread pudding for everyone.

"We had a visitor!" Justin exclaimed, as Jared pulled a drawing out of his pile. "A fireman. We got to try on his gear. And practice 'stop, drop and roll.'"

The boys were about to demonstrate, when Maggie cruised by with a trayful of dirty dishes. "No rolls in this place, kiddos, except for your father's most excellent biscuits."

The boys giggled as they clambered up into a booth. Morgana snuggled in next to them. She had her hair tied up in two ponytails, with big red-and-green bows topped with jingle bells, and she took every opportunity to toss her head and draw the boys' attention to her. "Gabriel, honey," she said, "do you want to know what I did today?"

Except for her appearance right now at the diner, he hadn't given her a thought since he'd dropped her at the Y the night before. "Tell me," he said, in an attempt to be polite, as he placed the desserts on the table.

"I walked over to the rec center. Lynn let me work in the storeroom, and I finished all the snow-flake costumes for the pageant. Boy, will Olivia be surprised. And the costumes are so awesome, if I do say so myself. You two—" she tickled both twins "—will be jealous you don't get to wear them."

"None of the boys want to be snowflakes," Justin protested.

"I don't know. I don't hear Jared saying he doesn't want to be a snowflake…."

"I'm saying it for him," Walter interjected.

"I'm just teasing, Walter." Morgana winked at Jared. "Jared knows that."

"Ms. Marshall says it's not nice to tease," Justin declared.

"I don't think she meant me." Morgana pouted.

"Try the bread pudding, Morgana," Gabriel said, hoping to head off a childish tiff. Then, to Walter he said, "You want me to fix you a takeout bag for supper? I made calamari."

"Gawd, no."

"Well, Marmaduke made a really *traditional* stuffed roast pork."

"That sounds delish." Morgana piped up, seemingly revived by the bread pudding. "We'll pick it up on our way back from skating."

"I never agreed to skating," Walter groused.

"Then you can go visit your friends at the VFW and I'll take the boys."

"We do wanna skate, Grampa," Justin said around a mouthful of dessert.

"Can I get in the loop?" Gabriel asked. "I know I'm only the dad."

"And a terrific dad you are." Morgana simpered, clearly buttering him up so that he would take her side. "So wouldn't you like your sons to be out in the fresh air, getting some exercise? On my way back from the rec center, I stopped by the skating rink. It's free to get in. We'd just have to rent skates. I've got enough to cover it." She propped her chin on her hands and batted her eyelashes. "Please, baby? Pretty, pretty please?"

Walter snorted, and the boys stared at their father as if seeing him in a new light.

"Morgana, do you even know how to skate?"

"You're looking at the pride of the Watkin's Circle roller rink. How much different can ice-skating be?"

"Please, Dad?"

"All right. But remember to wear your hats and scarves and mittens."

"Oh, Gabriel," Morgana cooed, "don't be such an old lady. We'll be fine. Won't we, boys?"

The twins nodded, but Walter looked doubtful. "I'll just stop in the VFW for a minute, and then I'll come watch you skate."

"Goody!" Morgana batted her eyelashes at Walter. "I always do better with an audience. Does anyone have a quarter? I wanna play 'Santa Baby' on the jukebox."

Later, when his family had cleared out and he had bused their table, Maggie stopped next to him, ostensibly to retie her apron. "You think that's such a good idea, leaving her alone with them?" she asked, nodding in the direction of the door. "She's nothing but a kid herself."

"She means well," Gabriel replied, hoping he was doing the right thing, and knowing how limited his options were these days.

"She means something, all right," Maggie muttered as she took the tray of dirty dishes out of Gabriel's hands. "Where you're concerned, that is. Sure hope you can handle her."

So did he. So did he.

ADRIENNE QUINCY WOULD make a terrible poker player. With an expression on her face that clearly announced she had the winning hand, Robert's mother sat across a classroom table from Olivia.

"What do we need to discuss today?" Olivia asked, dreading the answer.

"I think you're being way too hard on Robert," his mother replied. "In fact, I think I could say you're picking on him."

Although it wasn't the answer Olivia had expected, it formed an inauspicious start. "Why would you think I'm picking on him?"

"Well, for starters, you always take Jared Brant's side in any issue the boys have." She smiled. Quite insincerely. "Isn't Jared Gabriel Brant's son?"

"One of the twins, yes." Keeping her expression neutral, Olivia proceeded with extreme caution. "I have intervened with the boys quite a few times. And each time the *issue* was the same. Robert was teasing—"

"Oh, let's not get all politically correct. Sometimes kids tease. Boys will be boys. Real boys develop a thick skin."

That mother lion instinct kicked in. "Let me assure

you Jared Brant is a real boy. One who's experienced some serious problems no adults should have had to face. You've heard of Hurricane Katrina?"

"Oh, that excuse. That was two years ago. If Jared hasn't spoken by now, maybe you should transfer him to a special-needs class."

Olivia began to seethe inwardly, but she clung to her professionalism. "I can only discuss Jared as his interactions pertain to your son."

"Well, let me tell you how his interactions pertain to my son." The woman leaned across the table. "Your obvious favoritism toward Gabriel Brant's sons is shortchanging the rest of the kids in your classroom."

"I've taught kindergarten for ten years, and I don't play favorites." Olivia rose to show this meeting was over. "I teach each child according to his or her needs. In kindergarten most children need to learn they are not the center of the universe. They need to learn kindness and empathy, so that they'll be able to work with many different people throughout their lives."

"Struck a nerve, have I?" Adrienne Quincy rose, too. Slowly. "Perhaps if things don't improve, I may need to transfer Robert to the other kindergarten class. Of course, I'd have to provide a *detailed* explanation for my request."

"One other thing you need to know about me. I don't respond to blackmail."

Whether that was true or not, Olivia now found herself alone in the room and shaking.

CHAPTER TWELVE

NORMALLY, GABRIEL LEFT the diner after he'd prepared the last meal of the day and cleared up his work area. The waitresses then cleaned the dining room, after all the customers had gone, and Marmaduke came back to cash out and lock the place up. Tonight, however, Gabriel stuck around until the boss returned.

"What's up?" Marmaduke asked. "I thought you'd be long gone."

"I'm offering to lock up after you empty the register. I need a neutral space to talk to someone." The idea—the pressure—had been growing all day. "Somewhere private, where we can have a cup of coffee and iron out a few things."

Marmaduke raised one bushy eyebrow. "Sure," he said at last, the one word a huge relief to Gabriel. If it had been Walter, the old man would've immediately asked if Gabriel was in trouble.

While Marmaduke cleaned out the cash drawer and went over the receipts, Gabriel made a call from the pay phone.

"Hello?" Olivia's sleepy voice on the other end of the line made his pulse race.

"Hey, it's Gabriel. Are you in bed?" *Real stupid question.* He was a blundering idiot. "I mean, are you up for a cup of coffee? I'm at the diner. I could put on a fresh pot."

"I could use a jolt of caffeine." He realized her voice sounded not sleepy, but definitely bone weary.

"Bad day?" Damn. Why did he have to go and ask that? He had his own agenda for this meeting, and it wasn't domestic small talk.

"Bad day?" She sighed. "Something like that."

Okay, now he was worried. He'd gotten used to her being indefatigable. "Should I come get you?"

"No!" Her emphatic response led him to believe she might need neutral territory, too. "I can walk. I'll be there in a few minutes."

"I'll have the coffee ready." He hung up, wondering how tough he could be, if she was feeling low. Vulnerable. He didn't want to make her bad day worse, yet he needed to be tough. For his own sake.

"Good night!" Marmaduke called from the front door. "And good luck."

Good luck would have involved meeting Olivia the second time around, when Gabriel's life was back on track. When he had something to offer. Something more than significant debt, a room in his father's house, a job as a short-order cook and a situation with an ex even he didn't understand.

He'd finished making the coffee when he noticed Olivia standing outside the locked front door, her face framed by the huge Christmas wreath. Hands in her pockets, shifting her weight from foot to foot, she looked unsure of herself. How long had she been standing there?

Even after he opened the door for her, she remained outside. "Maybe this wasn't such a good idea," she said.

"Come on in. We need to talk."

She eyed the diner's empty interior. "How about getting your coat? I'd rather walk and talk."

"Have a heart, woman. It's gotta be in the teens out there, and I still have thin Southern blood flowing in my veins. Take pity on a man and get in here where it's warm."

Cautiously, she stepped inside, bringing an exotic fragrance with her—a light floral scent tinged with the sharp tang of frosty air. He thought of his boyhood and of finding snowdrops peeking up through the snow in the woods. Of feeling that he'd discovered a beautiful treasure. The memory was a powerful trigger.

"Make yourself comfortable," he said. "I'll get the coffee and a couple of baked apples I saved for us."

"No pecan pie?"

"No. I think I'm going to have to press Marmaduke for a pastry apprentice. I can't make those things fast enough to keep up with demand."

"Too bad. I was looking forward to a taste. Morgana says you make the best pecan pie in the whole world."

"She's given to exaggeration." Here it was. Olivia was handing him an opening. Morgana was one of the reasons Gabriel needed to make it perfectly clear that last night couldn't be repeated. *So take the damned opening,* he told himself.

He didn't. Because the dark circles under Olivia's eyes tugged at his resolve and made him want to take the time to find words that were honest without being hurtful.

He slid a tray with coffee and baked apples onto the corner table Olivia had chosen. Poured heavy cream over the apples.

"Marmaduke says he's gained ten pounds since you came to work for him," she said.

"The boss exaggerates, too. Besides—" Gabriel poured more cream on her apple "—a little indulgence, one cold night, isn't going to hurt you."

"If you're going to feel the guilt, you might as well enjoy the pleasure?"

"Something like that."

"If only it were that easy."

At the irony in her tone, he froze, realizing what they were saying. "What happened to make it a bad day?"

After such a perfect night.

"Oh, I don't want to talk about it," she replied, putting forth a cheeriness he sensed she didn't feel. With her spoon she scooped up a portion of apple and cream and tasted. "Mmm. If your pecan pies are better than this, no wonder Marmaduke's gained weight. Just let me enjoy it, while you tell me why you called this meeting."

Why had he called her here? To tell her, as much as he might wish otherwise, that he couldn't see her again. Couldn't—wouldn't—sleep with her again, because it wasn't fair to her. Because it distracted him from all he needed to do to provide for his boys.

So tell her.

He couldn't. Because she'd come to him tired and a little discouraged, for some reason. Because eating the simple dessert he'd made, she'd begun to relax visibly. He didn't want to ruin her improved mood. In fact, he felt a twinge of pride, knowing that he'd been able to give her some pleasure, to ease her weariness at the end of a hard day. If he was honest with himself, he'd have to say it would be nice—real nice—to take care of her on a regular basis. You couldn't blame a guy for dreaming.

"Gabriel?" She was staring at him. "What did you want to talk about?"

"The…twins." He suddenly realized Olivia was the one person he trusted in regard to his whole messed-up situation. He couldn't see her passing judgment. "Morgana. My father. The diner. My screwed-up life, in general." Once started, he couldn't seem to stop himself. "Us. You name it."

What was he doing? He had just let down his

defenses for the first time in years. He felt exposed. And treading on dangerous ground.

"Us?" Olivia felt her stomach do a little flip. "As in last-night us?" She sensed the brush-off coming.

Someone—several people, shivering and pantomiming drinking coffee—knocked at the restaurant door.

Gabriel stood and pointed at the sign in the window. "We're closed." When the people turned away, disappointed, he hit the bank of switches near the door, shutting off all the lights except the one directly over the table in the corner where he and Olivia were sitting. Creating a small private world.

As he sat down again, Olivia said, "You were talking about your life as messed up, and you included us."

"We're part of it, sure. Last night, a big part." He looked down into his coffee cup. "In fact, up until a couple minutes ago, I thought that was a huge chunk of the craziness. But…" Looking up at her, he seemed to have let his guard down. "I realize now you're caught up in my life in a dozen different ways. Starting with that summer when we were kids."

"It's strange you mention that. I was beginning to think that summer had no impact on you."

He held her with his penetrating gaze. "Olivia, you and your aunt were my refuge."

"I kind of had that feeling."

"My parents had a relationship I never understood," he explained. "My father was this kick-ass union steward over at the plant, and my mother was a stay-at-home mom. But there, she seemed to wield a strange power over him. He was absolutely devoted to her. I got the feeling he worried he could lose her at any moment."

This is the time to tell him, Olivia thought, but she couldn't bring herself to interrupt his narrative. To risk derailing his new openness.

"With Daniel and me, there was a clear delineation of rank. Daniel was my father's favorite. I was my mother's. That summer you and I were friends, Daniel went off to Arizona to Boy Scout camp. His absence seemed to throw my parents and me off balance. My mother was the same, but my father almost seemed jealous of me. I was only ten, but staying out of the house seemed like a good idea."

"A lot of pressure for a kid," she said, fiddling with the Santa and Mrs. Claus salt-and-pepper shakers. Wondering why real-life couples were never as uncomplicated.

"But with you and your aunt I could be myself," he continued. "I didn't have to live up to any macho standard."

"But you were so macho!" She smiled, remembering. "You were King Arthur and Mr. T, all rolled into one."

"Yeah. But I also felt safe, helping you and your aunt bake cookies. No one was going to tell me to get out of the kitchen and go play ball in the street like a real boy."

She suddenly felt a jolt of trepidation. "Is your father like this with the twins?"

"No. Not really. In fact, he's very protective of the boys. I only saw that one flare-up, when you came over with the recorder for Jared, but you stood up to him and he backed down. He respects you."

"You don't think he respects *you?*"

"No. Maybe that's why he's so protective of Justin and Jared. I'm sure he thinks I'm not up to the task of raising them."

"Maybe you're reading too much into it. Maybe all he wants is a second chance."

"I'd like to see the world from a kindergarten teacher's eyes. Life would be much simpler."

She was stung by his remark, but she wasn't about to let go of the unexpected dialogue they'd been sharing. "Just because I can see clearly doesn't make me simple."

"Sorry. I didn't mean it as an insult." He mashed the remains of his baked apple into a pool of cream, making a mess for which she would have chastised her students.

"May I make a suggestion?" she asked.

The corner of his mouth pulled upward. "Can I stop you?"

"Probably not, so here goes. Start with the attachment Walter seems to have for Justin and Jared. Accept it without second-guessing the reasons for it. Then try to forge a new relationship with your father. One that begins now. In the present. With the boys as a bridge."

"You make it sound so easy."

"I know it's not, but what's the alternative?"

He didn't answer, so Olivia persisted, leaning forward across the diner table to make her point, grazing his hand with her fingertips. "The last thing you need to do is overcomplicate the issue. You have complications enough with Morgana in town."

"You noticed," he replied drily.

"Have you had a chance to talk with her further? Has she told you what she wants?"

"I haven't had time to turn around, let alone have a heart-to-heart with Morgana. A chef's... A *cook's* hours aren't particularly conducive to raising a family alone." His amendment had a bitter tinge. "As much as I hate to admit it, Walter's been a big help. But what if Morgana hasn't really shown her claws? Although she says she realizes her lifestyle is less conducive to raising kids than mine, what if she wants them back, anyway? A judge might look at my setup here—complete with Walter's little field trips to the VFW—and side with the mother. Then there's the matter of how I reacted to becoming an instant dad. All a lawyer would have to do is interview a few of my friends and employees at the time, and the case for me as a disaster of a father is complete."

"But you're not a disaster of a father now. Believe me, as a teacher, I can tell in a very short time who takes parenting seriously and who doesn't. You're a good and loving father, Gabriel. Stop beating yourself up for however you felt when you got blindsided four years ago."

Two deep vertical lines appeared between his eyebrows. "I look at them now, I think of how much I love them now…and I feel guilty."

She understood his dilemma, and understanding created a fierce longing to be by his side. Part of the solution. "But you're getting way ahead of yourself, thinking Morgana's going to dig up all your past thoughts and use them against you. Besides, you're not alone in this. You have Walter. And you have me."

He couldn't have looked more startled.

"I mean…I'm the boys' teacher. As Walter picks them up every day, I can involve him more in the process. It's amazing how, in that short time right around dismissal, you can slip in a mini progress report and some suggestions for appropriate enrichment. I've been treating him more as babysitter. Maybe I can make him feel actively vested in their education. Make him see the two of you as a team."

"So you're not only a kindergarten teacher, you're a miracle worker?"

Was he going to call her a social worker? Did he still distrust her motives? She hesitated before making her next offer. "And Morgana, well, maybe she could use a friend."

He looked really dubious now, as he got up to retrieve the coffeepot from behind the counter.

"If not a friend, then maybe a gentle counselor," she said, as Gabriel refilled their cups. "She needs to realize how much parenting requires of a person. As a teacher, I can make her see the challenges pretty clearly."

"You'll never get her into your classroom, if that's what you're thinking. She hated school."

"I know. She told me. But she's helping with the pageant, and I was thinking of inviting her to my house Friday with my bunco group. To decorate my tree. Most of the women who come are parents. Morgana will get an earful, believe me. I don't mean to scare her off. But she needs to be able to make an informed decision."

"I should have known, when we planned all those mock battles that summer, that you'd turn into a major strategist later on in life."

She looked closely at him and could sense relief. She should have let him bask in it, but some naughty impulse residing somewhere to the right of her good conscience wouldn't let the matter drop. "When I said 'you have me,' you didn't think this was what I had in mind, was it?"

He narrowed his eyes and a slash of red cut across each chiseled cheekbone. "No."

"About last night…"

"I can't stop thinking about you," he said, so low that it sounded almost like a moan.

"Nor I you. So, what are we going to do about it?"

"You know what Walter says we should do about it?"

"Walter has an opinion about us?"

"Walter has an opinion about everything."

"Well, this one I have to hear."

"Walter thinks you and I need to get married."

She suddenly felt as if she'd broken the surface after being held underwater way too long. As instinctively as sucking in air, she replied, "Is that so outrageous?"

CHAPTER THIRTEEN

THE REST OF THE DINER seemed to fall away, leaving Gabriel and Olivia marooned in their small island of light.

"You've got to be kidding," Gabriel declared, stunned that he'd voiced Walter's opinion, and even more stunned that Olivia had considered it. "You don't think the idea of us getting married is outrageous?"

"Aside from the fact that a stable two-parent home would pretty much assure you'd get custody of Justin and Jared, and Morgana would get visitation rights, yeah, I was kidding."

"You weren't kidding." He couldn't believe she'd be willing to do this. "What would be in it for you?" He didn't mean to sound crass, but his experience led him to believe nobody did anything for nothing.

"The boys. A family." She spoke softly, but there was longing in her eyes. "You."

"Oh, I'm a prize, for sure."

"Don't put yourself down."

Another knock came at the restaurant door.

"We're closed!" Gabriel called out, without even looking. "We'd better get out of here."

He rose to clear the table. In the kitchen he quickly rinsed the dishes and stuck them in the dishwasher, then grabbed his windbreaker from its hook on the wall. Behind the counter he pulled the plug on the string of red-hot chili pepper lights looped over the specials board. "Come on. I'll walk you home."

After he'd locked the front door, they walked in an uncomfortable silence from the diner on Main Street to Olivia's house on Winterberry. As she fitted the key into her front door lock, he turned to go.

"I have to tell you something," she said, stopping him in his tracks. "Something you don't seem to know. Hennings is where you belong."

"Oh, really?"

She touched his cheek with her gloved fingertips. "Your pain won't let you see your path right now, but I can help ease the pain." She removed her hand, but held his gaze. "I understand loneliness."

He'd never imagined her lonely. Even though she'd grown up without parents, her aunt had been a devoted guardian. As a girl, Olivia had made friends easily. And when he'd come back to town this time, he'd found her at the center of a flurry of activity, liked and respected by all. He'd seen her as strong, and—if the truth was told—he'd seen her as somehow above him. Someone who didn't feel the hurt that life could dish out. Maybe all that activity, all those friends formed a convenient armor.

Her admission seared him.

Without thinking, he took her in his arms and kissed her. Kissed her as if he wanted to take away all her loneliness and replace it with a warmth and devotion he knew he couldn't provide. Not now. Not when his life was so fractured.

But in her arms, kissing her, he didn't feel fractured. In fact, he felt himself begin to heal. Felt as if being a man and a father and a lover might not be random conditions but parts of a whole. "I can't make promises," he breathed in her ear.

"For now, I'll settle for honesty," she said, pulling him even closer in an embrace that gave him strength.

"You want honesty?" He tried to speak as gently as possible. "You need to think of all you might risk by involving yourself with me."

Feeling dazed, he left her. And as he did, he knew one thing: he had to straighten things out with Morgana before he could think of his path or his future or whatever new possibilities might arise.

At Main Street he looked at the digital readout hanging over the drugstore entrance. Ten-thirty. Morgana would still be awake. He headed for the Y.

At the front desk he asked for her, but a buzz to her room got no response. The clerk said she hadn't seen her since that morning. He asked to use the desk phone, and called Walter. Walter said she'd left as soon as the boys were settled in bed—several hours earlier—adding, "Are you in trouble?"

No, he wasn't, but Morgana might be.

Newly clean and in a town with no particular friends other than himself and Walter, Morgana could fall prey to temptations. Even in a place the size of Hennings. At least she didn't have a car... Gabriel refused to think the mother of his children might already have found companionship equipped with wheels.

He set out on foot to check out the few bars within walking distance of the Y. At the Shamrock, when he described Morgana, the bartender laughed and said, "Oh, her. She's in the back room, cleaning everyone's clock."

This did not bode well.

Ready to kick ass and take names, Gabriel stormed into the back room, only to find Morgana at a table with five other people playing poker. In front of her, Morgana had a pile of chips three times the size of any other player's.

"Gabriel, honey!" Her smile was as wide as the Oklahoma sky. "Who knew they'd have Texas Hold 'em in New York!"

One of the players threw down his cards. "I'm outta here before she holds my mortgage." He looked at Gabriel. "You want in? Be careful. She might be blond, but she's no way near as...innocent as she seems."

"He knows that, silly!" Morgana giggled. "I *am* the mother of his children. Oops! Forget I said that!"

All eyes turned to Gabriel. Did he know these people? Would any of them have children in Justin and Jared's class? Now, to stay ahead of the jungle drums, Morgana and he would have to level with the boys.

"We need to talk," he said to her.

"That's the game, then," another woman at the table said. Her back had been toward Gabriel. Now, when she stood, he could see she was wearing a police uniform. "But all bets get settled on the sidewalk outside the bar." She clapped her officer's cap on her head. "This isn't a gambling establishment, you know." She looked directly at Gabriel. "And I'm off duty."

Still unsettled by Morgana's admission, Gabriel ignored the obvious hairsplitting. He stared at his ex, who squirmed in her seat like a naughty child. She avoided eye contact as she put on her jacket and followed the other players out of the bar to settle their bets. Under the streetlamp Morgana pocketed a large wad of bills.

Walking back to the Y, she broke the silence. "You know, you can be a big spoilsport sometimes."

"I didn't intend to be. I only came looking for you to see if you were okay. The reason we had to break the game up to talk is the fact you spilled a few rather important beans back there. To complete strangers. Before your own sons know."

"Oh, that. I'd pretty much decided I should level with Justin and Jared."

"Sorry, I missed that memo."

"Well, you might have gotten it, if you were ever around." Frowning, she pulled her jacket collar up around her ears. "But all you ever do is work, work, work. You know, your father could use a break now and then. And I could use some company."

"Hey, I work to support the boys. That means taking what comes along. The diner hours aren't the greatest, but the pay's good. And you were the one, when you blew into town without warning, who said I didn't need to entertain you."

"Duh. I was entertaining myself just now before you dragged me out of there." She pulled the wad of money out of her pocket and shook it at him. "I'll have you know tonight I won enough to pay my girlfriend back, and then some."

"You could've just as easily lost what you started with." Ask him about unexpected reversals of fortune. He'd become an expert.

"Me lose?" With a boastful swagger, she stashed the money back in her pocket. "Not likely. I'm good."

"So this wasn't your first game."

"Uh-uh. You heard the guy back there. I'm not as innocent as I look."

Didn't he know it.

"Although I think he almost said 'dumb,'" she continued with a frown. "Wouldn't he be surprised to learn I've won a couple of regional tournaments?

Enough to make Max nervous that I might leave the club. I use that as leverage to pick my hours, but I'm beginning to think I should quit the dance business altogether and go on the road with poker. Ride the Texas Hold 'em craze. A good-looking girl is always welcome at the table. But I'd kinda put that idea on the back burner till tonight. You know, coming to Hennings has been a real eye-opener in more ways than one."

"Morgana, back to the boys. How would they fit into this career move of yours?"

"Well, there wouldn't be any naked women involved, so maybe they could travel with me part of the year. It would be a real geography lesson."

Gabriel ground his teeth.

"I haven't worked out all the details."

Clearly.

"About the boys," he said, reining in his mounting frustration. "We have a more immediate issue. Telling them you're their mother."

She waved at a passing car driven by one of her newfound poker buddies. "I can't wait to see their faces. I bet they won't believe it. I mean, I'm really more like a big sister, don't you think?"

Yeah, one that needed a large dose of common sense before she could be handed the keys to the family car. "When do you want to tell them?"

"I'm planning to go back next Monday," she said, wrinkling her brow, as if concentrating on a mental date planner. "To pay back my girlfriend and straighten up some loose ends. And make a decision about what I'm going to do next. You know, this trip up north has turned into a real spiritual journey for me."

It took every ounce of strength Gabriel possessed not to roll his eyes. "When do you want to tell them?" he repeated.

"Let's tell them Sunday," she replied. "The day before I leave."

They'd come to the Y. He turned to face her. "There are a couple problems with that plan. One, the boys could find out beforehand from the kids of any one of the people around that poker table."

"Oh, pooh. Nobody at that table knew you. I asked. Besides, when are you free for a sit-down before Sunday? Most of the time you're gone in the morning before the boys are up and back at night after they're asleep."

He hated that she'd clearly processed that fact.

"Well, Mr. Workaholic? It's either Sunday or get together in the diner on your afternoon break and let who-knows-who in on the announcement."

"I'll ask Marmaduke for a few hours off. Because Sunday just isn't going to work. You already left the boys once." He held up his hand to stop her protest. "For good reasons, sure. But what are Justin and Jared going to think when you announce you're back, and then immediately take off again?"

"It wouldn't be *immediately*. It would be the next day."

"You don't understand how kids think. They operate in a different time frame than adults. They're going to feel lied to, then abandoned."

"But they like me. I've only been here three days and they really, really like me."

"That would make the betrayal even more painful."

"But I'd be back. I'd make sure they knew that."

"Morgana, you said you'd decided to tell them. What do you have to gain by waiting?"

"Dammit, Gabriel, don't pressure me! I hate it when guys pressure me. Let me at least sleep on it." With a flounce she headed up the Y steps, then turned. "And don't you go telling them without me, you hear? Your name may be on their birth certificates, but I'm still their mother. Their legal, biological mother. Even if they don't know it yet."

Feeling more frustrated by the minute, Gabriel walked home under a sky that threatened snow, but didn't shed a flake. The whole atmosphere was one of a storm brewing. Forgive him if he was, where storms were concerned, a little gun-shy.

As the past four years had unfolded, he'd become more and more certain that to gain sole custody of his boys he'd only have to find Morgana and have her sign the requisite papers. A no-brainer. He could more easily have predicted the fallout from Katrina than he could have this turn of events.

This turn of events, on top of Olivia's bombshell reaction back at the diner. Olivia. Her beautiful, understanding face came to mind. And his overwhelming attraction to her. He hadn't predicted that, either.

Hell, he wasn't doing very well in the prediction department.

Then he thought of what Olivia had said about the two of them marrying. How it would establish a solid home for the boys. He could have custody, while Morgana had visitation rights. Olivia hadn't said it, but if he and she married, they would then become the emotional levee against Morgana's comings and goings.

Maybe Walter's bull-in-the-china-shop suggestion wasn't so far off the mark, and who in his right mind could have predicted that?

When he entered his father's kitchen, the old man was waiting. Scowling.

"I don't want to discuss it," Gabriel said, and went straight upstairs to check on his boys.

CHAPTER FOURTEEN

OLIVIA SMACKED THE snooze button on her bedside clock. She never dawdled in the morning, but she hadn't slept a wink the night before. That made two nights in a row. Here it was Wednesday, and she was about to begin the school day on empty. Well, not exactly empty. Her head was full of thoughts of Gabriel and their last conversation.

Why had he brought up Walter's suggestion that they get married? Was he seriously fishing, or had he expected her to dismiss it as ludicrous?

Well, the idea wasn't ludicrous.

Oh, yeah? Was she certifiable?

Gabriel had asked her what she expected to gain by a marriage of convenience, and she'd answered, the boys, a family—and him. He'd also asked her to think of what she might risk.

An orphan's longed-for sense of stability came to mind. Maybe her strictly professional self—always doing what was right and what was expected—had been serving to protect that little girl who, despite a kind aunt, friends and a career, forever felt as if she was making her way alone in the world. Did she really want to risk the emotional safety she'd painstakingly stockpiled for a man whose life was unsettled, to say the least?

The alarm rang again—and she hit the snooze again. She was going to be late for school, but for once she didn't care. Then she thought of her twenty-three charges. Of course she cared. Yet what good was she if she couldn't focus?

And how could she focus with Gabriel on her mind?

As too many questions tumbled through her overtired brain, Olivia pulled the pillow over her face and screamed. It felt so good that she screamed again, this time adding some excellent kindergarten-tantrum kicks that landed her covers on the floor. She really didn't want to be an adult today.

And why should she? That tiny good-conscience voice whispered a reply, *Maybe because the entire town sees you as "sensible Ms. Marshall."*

"Predictable Ms. Marshall," she said aloud, throwing off the pillow and sitting up. "Boring Ms. Marshall!" she shouted at the top of her lungs.

Right then and there, she knew she wasn't reporting for duty today. Let a substitute handle the color green, the number sixteen, the *ch* blend and the desert environment.

She was going to stay home and try to figure out how her tidy life suddenly had gone astray.

It was too late to ask for a personal day off, but

she already had so many unused sick days that, at this rate, she'd probably be able to retire five years early. She called the sub desk and told them she wouldn't be in. She didn't even offer up a fake cough.

When she got off the phone, she felt a rush of exhilaration. Liberation. For the first time in her entire teaching career, she was about to play hooky. She immediately went downstairs and devoured half a bag of Oreo cookies for breakfast, without a single attempt to rationalize them with a glass of milk. Feeling defiant, although slightly nauseous, she stumbled into the solarium to feed Burt.

"Boring Ms. Marshall!" he called in greeting. In her voice.

"Behave," she admonished, cleaning his water cup and replenishing it with fresh water. "And don't think you're watching talk shows and soap operas all day. I'm home and I control the remote."

"Bossy woman," he replied in Gabriel's voice.

"Be nice."

What was sadder than a single woman with a houseful of cats? A single woman who stooped to argue with her parrot roommate.

By eight o'clock Olivia had finished the bag of Oreos. By nine she'd cleaned the oven. By ten she'd painted her toenails red. By eleven she'd begun to wonder if she hadn't traded one Boring Ms. Marshall for another Boring Ms. Marshall. And had she solved all the riddles of her life? No.

The doorbell rang.

She wouldn't have answered it, except Burt squawked, "Who is it?"

"Morgana Starr! I brought you some chicken soup."

Tissues wadded between her toes, Olivia hobbled to the front door. When she opened it, Morgana exclaimed, "Boy, did I get here in the nick of time. You look awful." Stepping into the foyer, she thrust a covered container of soup at Olivia. "It'll be good. Gabriel made it."

"I don't understand. How did you know I was sick?"

Morgana wriggled out of her jacket. "I don't know what it is about Hennings, but I just can't seem to sleep late. Maybe it's the clean air. Anyway, I usually wander over to Walter's midmorning. He has premium cable and the Y doesn't. He and I have a cup of coffee and a doughnut. Or two. If I'm not careful, I'm gonna weigh a ton. Well, today he says you weren't in the classroom when he dropped the boys off at school. A sub was there. Freaked them out, I guess. Justin and Jared, not the sub and Walter."

"Did they stay in class? Justin and Jared?"

"Yeah, I guess Walter calmed them down. He's real good with the boys. Sorta grumpy on the outside, but a cream puff on the inside. So, when I get to his house today he tells me you're sick, and I think, 'Gee, I can play Clara Nightingale,' so I stop by the diner for the soup. And here I am. Now that

Gabriel knows you're sick, I bet he sends over supper, too." She looked down at Olivia's bright red toenails. "You want me to do your fingernails? I have a real steady hand."

"Sure." So why shouldn't she spend the morning with the mother of the children of the man she'd slept with? Good God, could her life get any more confusing? "Let's go in the kitchen. It's warmer there."

"Wow," Morgana sighed as Olivia led the way down the hall.

When Olivia turned back, she saw her peeking into the living room and the solarium beyond, her eyes as wide as a child's on Christmas morning. "Do you live here alone?"

"Yes." Now, why didn't she want to admit to the parrot?

"You could fit my whole apartment in this one room. I don't know what I'd do with all this space." She caught up with Olivia. "This is a house built for lots of kids. Do you have kids?"

"No."

"I suppose you heard through the grapevine about my kids. Mine and Gabriel's."

"I didn't hear anything through the grapevine, but I guessed the first day I met you." Olivia began to wonder if this visit had another agenda beside the stated one. "They look just like you."

"Thanks. Wow! This kitchen is bigger than the one at the Y. Did you ever think of opening a bed-and-breakfast?"

"That would be a little difficult. Because I already have a full-time job," she added, when Morgana looked confused.

"Teaching, yeah. Gosh, if you left teaching, there would be some heartbroken kids, that's for sure. Justin and Jared are really sweet on you."

Not sure where this conversation was going, Olivia made herself busy ladling out a bowlful of the chicken soup. She needed something besides cookies in her stomach. "They're special boys."

"That's Gabriel's doing, for sure. So, where's your nail polish?"

"Next to the sink. Do you want a bowl of soup?"

"Nah." Morgana retrieved the polish. "I ate two and a half doughnuts at Walter's."

Olivia zapped her soup for a minute in the microwave, then brought the bowl to the table. She carefully began to eat with her left hand while Morgana applied polish to the right.

"You have nice nails."

"Thanks."

"From what I hear, from the boys and Walter and the people working on the pageant and the folks down at the Shamrock, you're just really nice all over."

"Sometimes nice gets boring," Olivia replied, startled at her own response.

"Don't say that. Nice gets you a good, steady job. Nice gets you guys who don't give you a black eye. Nice makes little boys want you for their mother." She stopped applying the polish.

"Morgana, have you told the boys you're their mother yet?"

"No. Gabriel thinks we should do it soon. Before I go back to Oklahoma next week."

"He's right."

"I know. But it would be so much easier to tell them if we could also tell them we were getting back together."

Olivia's heart sank. "Is that what you want?"

"I think I could really love a guy like Gabriel."

Like Gabriel. Not necessarily Gabriel.

"We did make beautiful babies," Morgana said, her voice wistful.

"Yes, you did." There was no counterargument to that. Suddenly, Olivia wondered exactly where she fitted into this picture. Even if there was chemistry between Gabriel and her, could she—should she—play the other woman, if there was the slightest chance he could make a family with the mother of his children? What was best for Justin and Jared?

Morgana sniffed loudly, then tossed her hair. "Here, let me do your other hand."

As Morgana worked on her left hand, Olivia blew on the polished nails of her right. It gave her an excuse not to talk.

"Being a teacher and all, you know most everybody's business in town, don't you?" Morgana asked at last.

"I know almost everybody. But I try to stay out of their business. Why do you ask?"

"Do you know if Gabriel's hooked up with anybody yet?"

Olivia felt her cheeks flame red, and Morgana noticed. "What? Don't kindergarten teachers know about that stuff?" she teased.

"No. Yes. I mean, because I teach their children, I try not to pry."

"You *are* nice."

Then why did Olivia feel so guilty?

Morgana studied her face. "I'm not sure how I'd feel if I found out Gabriel had someone. I mean, there goes my little dream of a reunion, but maybe him finding a partner to help with the boys would ease my conscience if I don't stick around full-time."

"It seems as if you have a lot of serious thinking to do." It was the only comment Olivia could find to offer. Who knew that she and this woman would have so much in common?

"There." Morgana put the finishing touch on Olivia's last nail. "If you had any green polish, I could put tiny holly leaves on for an accent."

"Sorry. Red's as daring as I get."

"Hey, did Regina or Lynn tell you I finished the pageant costumes?"

"Yes, both did. That's wonderful. We can't thank you enough."

"Well, do you have anything else for me to do?" Morgana screwed the cap on the polish. "I've got five more days in town, and I get bored easily."

"I can't think of anything at the moment, but I

was going to ask you if you wanted to join my bunco group on Friday."

Morgana hesitated. "My game's really Texas Hold 'em."

"It's not so much the game as the company. We'll play a little bunco, drink a lot of schnapps and decorate my Christmas tree."

"Is it couples?"

"No. It's a bunch of rowdy women."

"Oh."

"Lynn will be here, and you'll know me."

"Can I get back to you?" Morgana stood up.

"Sure. Thanks for the soup. And the manicure."

"I can show myself out. Once that polish dries, you should get back in bed. You really don't look so hot."

Alone again, Olivia gazed at herself in the downstairs bathroom mirror. She didn't look *that* bad.

Morgana seemed so transparent. What you saw was what you got. Or was it? How much had this visit been a simple act of kindness, and how much had it been a reconnaissance mission?

Suddenly, Olivia wished herself back in the classroom, where a smile was just a smile and a bite was just a bite.

AS SOON AS THE LUNCH RUSH subsided, Gabriel packed up an individual serving of the lasagna he'd made as the supper special.

Marmaduke looked up from a North Carolina re-

tirement community brochure he'd been reading at
his desk in the closet-size office off the kitchen.
"That smells good," he said, "but I'm surprised it
only took two and a half weeks for you to come
down to our level. Diner comfort food."

Gabriel had opened his mouth to say there
wasn't anything wrong with a well-made lasagna,
when the boss gave a lopsided grin. "I'm just
raggin' you. You could advertise poached eggs and
we'd run out in a heartbeat. You've established a
following. With good reason. Your converts'll still
keep busy discussing what the hidden seasonings
might be."

Shaking his head, Gabriel loaded the prepared
trays of food onto the steam table. The real reason
he'd made this particular dish was because he could
have made it in his sleep. His mind was so filled
with thoughts of Olivia and the kids and Morgana
and even Walter that he couldn't handle anything
more complicated. Besides, the waitresses could
cut up and serve the lasagna while Marmaduke
filled in with the short orders. If he'd agree.

"Hey, boss, I need the rest of the day off."

Marmaduke looked at the already made supper
special with dawning understanding.

"I wouldn't ask, but I have to settle a really important matter with my boys."

"Sure." Marmaduke grew serious. "I know what
it's like to try and raise a family and cook, too. The
hours. Let me tell you, the juggling act never ends.

My daughter's grown now, with kids of her own."
He waved the retirement community brochure at
Gabriel. "She wants my wife and me to move to
North Carolina so we won't be strangers to the
grandkids." He came out from behind his desk to
tie on an apron. "Go. We'll manage here. Although
I might just take credit for that lasagna."

Gabriel scooped up the package of food and his
windbreaker. He'd just have a minute to drop off the
dinner at Olivia's before getting to school by dismissal time.

Morgana had had a night to think about revealing herself as the boys' mother. Deciding he wasn't
going to let her stonewall any longer, Gabriel
planned to meet her and Walter at the school. Then
they were going to walk home as a family and clear
the air. Although maybe Walter and his pyrotech-
nics didn't need to be a part of it.

It only took a few minutes to walk the block
from the diner on Main to Olivia's front porch on
Winterberry. Hoping she was well enough to answer the door, Gabriel rang the bell. He supposed
he could have left the dinner with her neighbors,
asking them to deliver it later, but he felt the need
to see her before he had that heart-to-heart with
Morgana and the boys. Unaccountably, Olivia had
become his stable base.

When she opened the door, he was sorry he'd
disturbed her. She stood wrapped in an oversize
red robe that made her seem small and fragile.

"Brr!" Clutching the robe to her, she shivered. "It's freezing! Come on in."

"I'm sorry," he said, entering the house on a rush of frigid air. He held out the dinner. Sick or not, she looked beautiful to him. "I shouldn't have disturbed you. But I wanted to make sure you had something that would stick to your ribs for supper."

"Thank you," she said. "Morgana thought you might be by. She brought soup earlier."

So that's where the soup had gone. Morgana hadn't explained, and he'd assumed it was for the boys' supper. What was his ex up to?

"Thank Marmaduke," Olivia said, almost shyly, "for letting you deliver this."

"I took the rest of the day off. I'm on my way to intercept Morgana and Walter at school. We're going to tell the boys Morgana is their mother."

Olivia suddenly seemed distraught. "I'm so sorry I wasn't at school today. If I'd only known…oh, my. To handle this news, the boys should have had a secure classroom routine as a buildup. Instead they had a sub."

"You couldn't have known." Still, he was grateful for her instinctive concern for the boys' wellbeing. He'd come to expect no less. "Hell, last night at ten-thirty I didn't know I'd be having this conversation with them this afternoon. Morgana kind of went public last night. Without thinking things through."

"Then go. Hurry. And please let me know how

things work out, or if there's anything I can do to help Justin and Jared cope."

She didn't seem to know it, but she'd helped just by being Olivia.

He didn't have time to tell her as much. Only time enough to brush a fleeting kiss across her forehead before jogging down Winterberry Street to the school. Morgana and Walter were already retrieving the boys.

"Daddy!" Justin shouted. "Ms. Marshall's sick. Jared cried. Ow!" Jared had landed a kick to his brother's ankle. "We made her get-well cards," Justin said, rubbing his leg and casting a baleful look at his twin. "Can we take them to her?"

Morgana gave Gabriel a warning glance.

"Ms. Marshall needs her rest so she can get back in the classroom. But I'll slip those in her mail slot later. Right now I'm coming home with y'all. How does popcorn and my world-famous hot chocolate sound?"

"Yummy!" Justin slipped his mittened hand into Gabriel's. "But how come you're not at the diner?"

Gabriel looked at Walter. "I thought your grampa needed a break. I hear it's been awhile since he's seen his buddies down at the VFW."

Walter slitted his eyes. "You trying to get rid of me?"

"You turning down a beer with the guys?"

Morgana looked increasingly nervous, but she tried to shoo Walter away. "Gabriel's right. Don't look in a horse's mouth for a gift."

"You two know what you're doin'?" Walter asked.

Morgana looked to Gabriel.

"Yes," he said.

"What about supper?" The old man was hanging on by his fingernails.

"I'll have it ready at six. I bet even you could use a break from SpaghettiOs."

"We'll save you some popcorn and hot chocolate, Grampa," Justin promised.

With a gentleness Gabriel hadn't known his father had in him, Walter lay a hand each on the boys' heads. "Grampa loves you," he said, before limping off toward his "country club."

Jared slipped his hand into Gabriel's free one. But where Justin was hopping about in anticipation, Jared was very still. Very solemn.

The awful expression "lambs to the slaughter," came to Gabriel's mind.

CHAPTER FIFTEEN

BACK AT 793 CHESTNUT, Gabriel made popcorn and hot chocolate while the twins helped Morgana find mugs and bowls. Morgana kept up a steady stream of silly chatter, but both boys were quiet, looking often to their father. Clearly, they suspected having him home in the afternoon meant something unusual was afoot.

In their short lives, surprises had not always been pleasant.

Finally, when all four were settled around the table, Gabriel took a deep breath. "Do you remember when I told you about your mother?"

"How she got sick and had to go away," Justin replied. "Ms. Marshall's sick. Is she gonna hafta go away?"

"No, honey," Morgana said. "This isn't about Ms. Marshall. Now pay attention."

Gabriel could imagine how differently Olivia would have handled this.

Before he could think of the next step, Morgana jumped in. "Well, your mom isn't sick anymore.

And she's come back. Haven't you guessed? I'm your mother."

The boys' eyes grew wide and uncertain. "But you told us you were Daddy's friend," Justin said, his tone implying clearly that the adults had lied.

"Moms and dads can be friends, too," Gabriel replied.

Frowning, Jared poked his brother in the ribs, and Justin responded for the both of them. "So Ms. Marshall isn't going to be our mom?"

Gabriel glanced at Morgana, who seemed as startled as he was. "What gave you the idea Ms. Marshall was going to be your mom?" he asked.

"Grampa said so." Justin looked sideways at Morgana. "Was he wrong?"

"I thought something was going on between you two," Morgana said, her tone petulant.

"Guys!" Gabriel didn't know how he was going to find the exact, honest words to explain the already convoluted relationship between himself and Olivia. "I know you like Ms. Marshall—"

"We love her," Justin amended.

"Okay, then." Gabriel began again. Morgana glaring at him didn't make his explanation easier. "I think because Grampa likes her, he was doing a little wishful thinking."

"My mama," Morgana interjected, "used to say, 'Wishing never made it so.'"

Poor Morgana.

"So, if you're our mom," Justin asked, "are you gonna live with us now?"

"Would you like that?"

"Grampa already says his house is bustin' at the seams with all of us here." He looked down at his hands in his lap. "I don't know if you would fit."

"Well," Morgana huffed, "where was he planning to put Ms. Marshall?"

"Morgana…" Gabriel raised his hand to stop this childish escalation. "We need to talk about Monday."

"Why? Oh, yeah, that's when I'm leaving." Her bull-in-the-china-shop approach made Walter's methods seem almost subtle. When the boys did a double take, she fluttered her eyelashes. "Gabe, honey, do we have to go there right now? This is a lot for the kids to take in."

Small steps. Maybe she was right. "Okay."

"All right," she said, turning to the twins. "What do you want to call me?"

"Besides Morgana?"

"You can still call me Morgana, until you feel comfy with something else. Mama makes me sound like your grandmother, but I like Mommy." She beamed at Gabriel. "Mommy and Daddy. Sounds good."

"May we be 'scused?" Justin asked, pushing his half-empty popcorn bowl to the center of the table.

"Yes," Gabriel said, before Morgana could protest. "Why don't you two go to your room and draw a picture for…your mother."

"Yessir." Two solemn little boys left the kitchen.

Morgana pulled her own little-girl face. "Geez, that didn't go like I expected."

"They'll be okay. But we need to give them time to process what they've heard."

"You know, I would've thought news like this would've made Jared say something. I gotta admit, sometimes his silence creeps me out."

How the hell had he gotten himself involved with this woman? Gabriel wondered. Babies hadn't been on his mind at the time, that was for sure.

"Listen to what you're saying," he told her, trying to keep his anger in check. "Right now, this is more about the boys than about you. They've been through so much trauma." Damn, even Walter understood that. "They must wonder if they're ever going to stand on solid ground."

"They seemed to like me better as just your friend."

How could he get through to her? "After four days with you around, they formed an idea of who you were in relation to their world, and now we're asking them to radically change that image. It's tough."

"I guess." She began breaking popcorn kernels into tiny crumbs. "Maybe I'm just not cut out for this motherhood gig."

"I'll be honest with you. Parenthood isn't easy. You have to commit to it."

"How am I supposed to commit to it when people are trying to sabotage me?"

"What are you talking about?"

"Tell me one thing. Is Walter the only one who's been thinking Olivia Marshall would make a good mother for my kids?"

Gabriel didn't want to admit it, but the thoughts he'd been having about Olivia hadn't been strictly parental.

OPENING THE DOOR TO Walter Brant, Olivia wondered how many visitors a supposedly sick girl should expect in one day.

"I know Morgana brought you soup," he said, tapping his breast pocket, "but I brought you the real deal. Can I come in?"

"Be my guest." She wanted to ask him what he knew of the boys' reaction to Gabriel and Morgana's announcement, but she resisted the impulse. She'd wait for Gabriel to tell her, instead.

Once in the foyer, Walter shook himself out of his coat, but not before retrieving the flask from his pocket. "It's some cold out there! Better bring in your brass monkeys, is all I can say."

"Brass monkeys!" Burt shouted.

"Either that's your parrot," Walter said with a wink, "or my son's got competition." He held up the flask. "Glasses?"

"What brings you by?" Olivia asked, leading him to the kitchen, as she had Morgana. As if they were all one big family, whose comings and goings were daily occurrences. "I thought maybe you'd be part of…the meeting."

"The big reveal, you mean? No, I realize the kids need to do this on their own. I'd probably say something I'd regret later. Now that my grandsons are living with me, I'm trying not to do that so much."

Olivia still didn't know why he'd chosen her house in which to hang out for the duration. She got two short glasses down from the cupboard. "Ice?"

"Are you crazy?" Walter poured two fingers of what smelled like brandy into the glasses. "If this doesn't put a little holiday cheer in you, I don't know what will. Bottoms up."

Why not? Not really sick, she hadn't taken any medication. Maybe the brandy would break up the Oreos that were still sitting like a lump in the bottom of her stomach.

Having thrown back his drink, Walter fixed her with a flinty stare. "So, you gonna let Morgana move in and take over?"

"I...I don't really think it's any of my business."

"Hmm," Walter replied, as if he didn't believe her.

"I want what's best for the boys," she added sincerely.

"You and me both."

The doorbell rang. Could that be Gabriel? She rose to answer it when the doorbell rang again. More insistently this time.

"Hold your horses!" Burt squawked.

Walter shook his head. "There's as much traffic here as at my house."

She hurried to the door, only to find Justin and Jared on the porch, their eyes red and their noses running. "Where's your dad?"

"Talking to Morgana." Justin ran a mittened hand under his nose. "She's our mother now." He didn't look happy about it.

"What've we got here?" Walter appeared in the kitchen doorway. "A couple of runaways?"

"Grampa!" The boys ran to him, and he scooped them into his arms. "You said Ms. Marshall could be our mom." Justin's declaration bordered on accusation, and Walter looked a little sheepish. "We came to ask her if she can still be. Eric Sedley has two moms."

"Hey, where'd you get the dirt on your shoes?" Walter asked, examining Jared's feet, as if that might give him an excuse not to answer the question.

"We mighta run through a garden."

"Then sit down and take them off. Ms. Marshall runs a clean house."

The boys sat on the floor, and Walter helped Jared take off his shoes while Olivia undid Justin's laces.

"I've only known you a short time," Olivia said, trying to look stern, but melting inside. "It's pretty soon for me to make such a serious decision as being a mom."

"We've only known Morgana four days."

Okay, so that wasn't the tack to take. "Does your father know where you are?"

"No, ma'am."

"Then let's call him, so that he doesn't worry."

Eyeing the empty glasses on the table, Jared nudged Justin. "Can we have something to drink?" Justin asked. "We ran the whole way and we're thirsty!"

Walter cleared his throat.

"Please?"

"I have milk, juice or water," Olivia replied, "but first, let's make that call to your father."

Walter punched the numbers on his cell phone, then let Justin explain to Gabriel where they were. "He'll be right over," Justin said, flipping the phone shut. "Now can we please have some juice?"

Olivia looked squarely at Walter. Why hadn't he offered to save Gabriel a trip and walk the boys home? He shrugged.

While she poured apple juice all around— despite Walter's look of dissatisfaction at the new amber liquid in his glass—the twins settled at her table as if they belonged there. "This is a very big house," Justin remarked, looking around. "If we lived here we wouldn't be bustin' out the seams."

Strange, but until right now, Olivia had never thought of the rambling Victorian as too big for just one woman and a parrot.

"June is bustin' out all over!" Burt sang from the other room.

"Can we see the parrot?" Justin asked after finishing his juice.

"Yes, you may."

"Grampa, did you meet Burt?"

"No. Ms. Marshall and I hadn't gotten to those introductions yet."

"Come on, then." Justin tugged on Walter's sweater. When Jared nudged him, Justin added, "But watch your language."

Walter chortled. "Who knew I'd be cleaning up my act at this stage of my life?"

Olivia let the boys take Walter into the solarium, while she put the empty glasses in the sink. It wasn't that she didn't want to be a part of their visit with Burt. It was that she wanted a private moment to relish the presence of children in her house. Especially the presence of these particular children. She feared that as much as they—and their grandfather—might want her and Gabriel to marry, Gabriel had too much to deal with right now to even consider such a crazy prospect. And as much as she already knew that she wanted him, she didn't want to stand in the way of the boys forging a loving relationship with their natural mother.

The doorbell rang again. Unless it was Adrienne Quincy wanting Olivia to account for all this activity, it should be Gabriel. "Hi," she said, opening the door and feeling unaccountably shy.

"Hi." Amid silly sounds coming from the solarium, Gabriel stepped into the foyer and Olivia's world felt complete. Odd how she'd never found it lacking before.

"The boys and your father are visiting with

Burt." She looked behind him to the porch. "Where's Morgana?"

"She headed back to the Y. In a snit. The boys' reaction to her news was underwhelming, to say the least. When she found out they'd headed here, I'm afraid she took it personally."

"I'm sorry."

"It's not your fault."

Perhaps not. But she hadn't discouraged the boys from feeling comfortable here. Feeling an attachment to her. "Surely Morgana realizes this is going to take some time."

"I tried to tell her a little about the adjustments I had to make after she first left me with the twins, but she's always been impatient. Always wanted instant results. And she's always had fragile self-esteem."

"This has got to be hard for her."

"Sometimes I wish you weren't so understanding."

Walter appeared with Justin and Jared. "You got something to say to your dad?"

"Sorry," Justin said, as Gabriel knelt before his sons.

"Do you understand how worried I was when I couldn't find you?"

Both boys nodded solemnly.

"You're not to take off without an adult."

"Yessir."

Gabriel rose and extended his hands, as if to go,

but Walter stepped forward. "I'll walk 'em home. So you can finish talking to Ms. Marshall."

"We saw candy canes in the other room," Justin added quickly.

"They're for my tree," Olivia replied, "but you may each have one."

"Grampa, too?"

"Yes."

"Thanks."

"Apple juice and candy canes," Walter muttered with a twinkle in his eye. "All this G-rated living has me twitchy." He retrieved his flask and the boys' shoes from the kitchen, then hustled the twins out the door. "Let's put these on outside, so we don't track any more dirt on Ms. Marshall's floor."

When Gabriel and Olivia were alone, Gabriel said, "Should I be insulted?"

"That he's pushing us together?"

"No." For a moment Gabriel seemed disconcerted. "That he's always playing the father-knows-best role."

"I think you're reading into it. From my conversation with him, I got the feeling he was trying to help. Trying to step back at times, even. To let you take care of your own business."

"Who were you talking to? Not my old man." He noticed the mistletoe hanging in the hall archway and sidestepped.

"Come in the kitchen. I'll make tea." She was still in her fuzzy robe and had on green slippers that curled up at the toes like elf shoes.

"But you're sick."

"Then you make tea for me," she replied. "We need to talk."

Oh, yeah, Gabriel thought. *Four words no man likes to hear.* Nonetheless, he followed her into the kitchen, where she plopped into a seat and looked up at him expectantly. Apparently, he really was to make tea.

Having put the kettle on to boil, he searched her cupboards for tea and found she had varieties from all over the world.

"When I taste them," she explained, "I can imagine myself in faraway places."

Her refrigerator, when he hunted for a lemon, didn't prove half as rewarding. "This looks like a college dorm fridge," he said, staring in disbelief at the shelves. Empty except for a carton of milk, an almost empty bottle of apple juice and the portion of lasagna he'd brought by earlier.

"The diner's always been my second kitchen," she said.

"That's strange. I haven't seen you in there much."

She blushed. "Lately I'm on a peanut butter kick."

He put two mugs of African rooibos tea on the table between them. "So what do we need to talk about?"

"I need to tell you something you may or may not know already. I think it explains why you and your father have always seemed to rub each other the wrong way. Maybe it explains why he's trying to make amends now. In a roundabout way, with Justin and Jared."

"What?" Having already been sideswiped by Morgana's reappearance, he wasn't looking forward to another family surprise.

"It's about your mother…."

"My mother? Why do you think you know something about my mother that I wouldn't know?"

"Because Aunt Lydia knew. And when she was dying, she unburdened herself to me."

"I'm not following this. Your aunt was a great lady, but she wasn't exactly my mother's age. I can't picture them as best buds."

"They weren't, exactly. But one day—you were probably in elementary school—Aunt Lydia found your mother in the library stacks, crying. She and your dad had just had a big row over how tough he was on you. Aunt Lydia took your mother into her office, made her some tea, and said it was as if the dam had burst. Your mother told Aunt Lydia that after your brother, Daniel, was born, but before you came along, she left your father for a while. Because of his temper."

"I never knew that."

"Walter went crazy missing them. Missing her. He threw himself into getting her back."

Gabriel could see his father doing it, too. No matter how tough he'd been with the boys, he'd adored Marjorie. Sometimes, it seemed, she'd had to get out of the house just for breathing room.

"Finally, she agreed to reconcile. Eight and a half months later, you were born."

Gabriel began to get it. "Walter wondered if I wasn't his."

"Perhaps. Your mother said he never confronted her. And Aunt Lydia thought he was afraid of what he might hear. He didn't want to force the issue, because he didn't want to risk losing your mother again."

"It drove him crazy that she seemed to favor me." Gabriel was stunned the old man had shown as much restraint as he had. "But I didn't feel she did. It's just that we had more interests in common."

"Yes. Aunt Lydia always said Daniel was a— how did she put it?—a much less subtle boy."

"He and the old man were cut from the same cloth, that's for sure," Gabriel replied, feeling less and more confused all at once. "Did my mother happen to tell your aunt whether I'm Walter's son or not?"

"No."

"This is a pretty hefty chunk of my history. Is there any reason you thought you should withhold it from me?"

"Initially, I didn't know whether you knew. And then, as we talked over the past couple of weeks, I realized you were operating in the dark."

He stood. "All these years I felt there was a missing piece. Something to explain the disconnect." Already frustrated with Morgana, he looked long and hard at Olivia. "I wouldn't expect you'd track me down and tell me, but I guess it would be reasonable to expect that, after the night we spent together, you'd level with me."

"I am leveling with you. Besides, I think you need to shore up the present with Walter, not pick away at the past."

"Oh, that's what you think? Why does everyone seem to have an opinion on how I should run my life?" He headed for the door.

"Don't kill the messenger," she replied, following him, her words bristling with irritation. "It encourages people to be less frank with you, not more."

He sure wanted to kill someone. Or, at the very least, blame someone. But whom? And for what? Wasn't this all ancient history? If so, why did it hurt so much?

"I need to go make supper for my kids," he said at last. "And a man who might or might not be my father."

Leaving Olivia openmouthed, Gabriel stormed home, prepared to have it out with Walter.

But when he entered the front door at 793 Chestnut, he understood some of the dilemma Walter must have faced upon Marjorie's return. Understood the anger that arose from frustration. Like Walter, Gabriel had a choice. He could force a confrontation, but if it turned out they weren't blood relatives, what would he do next?

"Daddy, look! We're putting a train around the Christmas tree."

"And before you yell at me," Walter grumbled, his head under the lowest branches, his skinny butt sticking up in the air, "I got it at the VFW rummage sale. For practically nothing. It would've been a crime not to take it."

"We're gonna make a town!" Justin crowed, as he and Jared piled up some empty boxes. It seemed Walter had provided brown paper bags and tape to cover them, and markers to turn them into buildings. "Wanna help?"

Even if Walter wasn't his biological father, how could Gabriel now take the man away from Justin and Jared? As he'd told Morgana, the twins had formed relationships since they'd arrived in Hennings. Could he step in now and try to explain that those attachments weren't what they'd imagined? Weren't real? Then again, what actually made them real?

Walter hadn't confronted Marjorie because he'd been afraid of losing her. Gabriel wasn't about to confront Walter now and risk his sons losing the only grandparent they'd ever known. Especially not before Christmas, when the twins finally felt at home. And when they were still tender from the discovery that Morgana was their mother.

But the confusion was beginning to eat at his stomach lining.

Not now, but sometime in the near future, Walter and he were going to have to clear the air.

CHAPTER SIXTEEN

THE LAST STORY Olivia had read to her students before sending them home for the weekend was Judith Viorst's *Alexander and the Terrible, Horrible, No Good, Very Bad Day.* Compared to Olivia's week so far, Alexander had it easy.

Gabriel and Olivia had gone from making love on Monday to having absolutely no communication by Friday.

It wasn't as if she hadn't tried to talk to him after revealing his mother's confidence earlier in the week. After he'd left her house, she'd called Walter's number, but either Walter or Gabriel was doing a lot of talking to someone else, or the phone was off the hook. On Thursday after school she'd dropped by the diner, but Gabriel was up to his elbows in flour in the kitchen. The dining room was so unusually busy with hungry Christmas shoppers, it wouldn't have been the appropriate place for a conversation, anyway. Thursday after the diner's closing time, she took a walk down to 793 Chestnut, but she could see through the front window that Morgana was there. Olivia then had to ask herself if she was pursuing the matter because she was concerned about Gabriel or concerned for herself. Because it looked as if she'd lost him? She couldn't come up with an honest answer, but she decided Gabriel was a man who didn't need to feel crowded. Especially not at this point in his life.

And she didn't need to appear desperate.

Because she wasn't.

So she'd backed off.

"ARE YOU COMING IN to help decorate your tree?" Lynn asked, sticking her head into the kitchen, where Olivia was taking a baked spinach and artichoke dip out of the oven. "Bunco has been abandoned, the schnapps is flowing and the tinsel is flying. Yet you're hiding out in the kitchen. Is everything all right?"

"I guess I haven't fully recovered from Wednesday."

Lynn shot her a look that said she knew exactly what kind of sick day that had been.

"Ladies, please, one at a time!" Burt insisted from the solarium.

The phone rang, saving Olivia from having to explain herself to Lynn. "Hello?"

"Olivia, this is Morgana. I just remembered you asked me to your party tonight. Sorry to call so late, but I can't make it."

"That's too bad. Are you okay?"

"Yeah. Great, in fact. You see, Gabriel didn't have to work the supper shift. So we've just finished eating, and we thought we'd take the boys to a movie."

"You don't have to explain."

"Oh, I think I do."

Olivia didn't know how to answer that.

"Don't worry, though," Morgana continued. "I know the pageant dress rehearsal is tomorrow. I'll have the boys at the rec center, ten sharp. Have fun with the girls." She rang off before Olivia could reply.

"What was that all about?" Lynn asked as raucous laughter issued from the living room.

"Morgana."

"Ah. The past couple days she's been all over town, complaining about how she hates to go back to Oklahoma and leave her boys. Clearly, she's bucking for some mother-of-the-week award. Although I think when she says 'her boys,' she's including Gabriel."

"So it appears." Every ounce of Christmas optimism drained out of Olivia.

Lynn scrutinized her face. "Tell me the rumors aren't true."

She didn't need to ask what rumors.

Lynn's eyes grew wide. "Have you lost your mind?"

Olivia slumped against the counter. "Just my heart."

"When did this happen? You've only known him—how long? A few weeks?"

"As an adult, yes. But tell me again when you knew Cary was the one?"

"The minute I laid eyes on him. Although…"

"I rest my case."

"What are you going to do?"

"I'm going to let him work things out with Morgana."

"You're a better woman than me. If there'd been a rival for Cary in the picture, I might now be just his pen pal from the Big House."

"But there were no kids involved. I might have been willing to turn my own life upside down, but I'm not about to mess with Justin and Jared's."

Lynn gave her a big hug. "Poor baby."

"No." Olivia pulled away from her friend with a determined smile. "That I'm not. So Mr. Right turned out to be Mr. Wrong. I still have a wonderful life. I really do. With terrific friends. And a tree that probably needs redecorating."

"Not to mention fifty kids who are raring to run through the pageant tomorrow with costumes and Ty Mackey's animals." Lynn grabbed a pot holder and the spinach dip. "Hey, Ty's single. Have you ever really looked at his butt? It's kinda cute. And you'd never have to buy eggs again. Although he does smell a wee bit like livestock."

Olivia let Lynn lead her into the living room, where the women were laughing and telling tales about recalcitrant husbands and hormonal teenage children and rabid bosses, and most of all, tales about themselves. Stupid or embarrassing or crazy things they'd done. And the heart of the matter was, they were laughing at themselves. And their listeners were groaning in sympathy, acknowledging that, in one form or another, they'd been there themselves. Olivia wasn't alone. She was merely human.

Encouraged, she accepted the shot of schnapps Lynn handed her and tossed it down, after which she took her Santa hat from the mantel, pulled it over her ears and then plopped down on the floor to string popcorn and cranberries before her rowdy guests ate most of the popcorn.

Tomorrow would be a better day.

BUT IT WASN'T.

It was only more hectic, leaving blessed little time to think. Saturday morning, the rec center was packed with excited children. The scenery crew was finishing up the backdrop, which looked like something out of Currier and Ives, and everyone had to watch out for paint cans. Ty Mackey, who trained all kinds of animals for TV and movie appearances, had two of his llamas, his potbellied pig, three of his sheep and a ten-year-old yellow lab under far better control than Lynn, Regina and Olivia had the kids.

"Careful with those costumes!" Lynn bellowed, as several dreidels threatened to collide with a row of Christmas trees, and the Kwanzaa candles pretended to melt a flurry of snowflakes. Even as Jack

Frost was trying to peek up Mrs. Frost's skirt. "Recorder choir, front and center!"

Jared jostled with the other children on the stage under the painted streetlamp, each child "costumed" in his own winter coat, hat and scarf. Complaints of "I'm hot!" filled the air.

"Get a good spot in front," Morgana urged Jared from the front row of the audience. "Back straight. Chest high."

Parents weren't allowed at the rehearsals, and this was why. They all became stage mothers. Olivia would have ejected Morgana, but technically, she was a costume volunteer, and Regina needed her there in case of wardrobe malfunctions. Biting her tongue, Olivia helped the kids find their marks on stage. Clutching his recorder, Jared sent her a wave and a sweet smile that made all the chaos worthwhile.

Once settled, the little choir performed "Jingle Bells" beautifully, except for the end, when someone audibly passed gas.

"Great job," Lynn called from the piano, having just accompanied them. "But next time recorders only. No other wind instruments allowed."

Trying not to grin, Olivia looked at her clipboard. "Up next, 'Sleigh Ride.'" She looked at the sea of happy faces around her and tried to remember what it was like to be a child. That thought helped her stay in the moment until the finale had the whole ensemble, Ty Mackey included, dancing in the aisles to "Jingle Bell Rock." And he did have a cute butt.

Olivia might be bruised, but she wasn't dead.

As parents began to crowd into the center to collect their children, Morgana came up to Olivia with Justin and Jared in tow. "I'm sorry I won't be here for the real show," she said, "but I have a few suggestions to give it a little Vegas pizzazz."

Flashing them a discreet thumbs-up, Olivia winked at Justin and Jared and didn't hear a word she said. Morgana might be the boys' mother, Olivia thought, but she was their teacher and she wasn't going anywhere.

"Just ask Gabriel for my number if you need to call me," Morgana said, apparently winding down. "You boys ready for a little Christmas shopping?"

"Yes'm," Justin replied.

"I'm taking them to get presents for their daddy and their granddaddy," Morgana explained, kneeling to zip the boys' jackets, tie their scarves and fuss over them in an overtly possessive way.

"Daddy needs a nice warm jacket," Justin said.

"Well, that's a boring gift," Morgana replied, tweaking his nose. "Let's go see if Hennings has something a little more exciting. Does he like video games?"

The woman was exhausting.

"Don't worry," Lynn whispered in her ear as she watched the three depart. "She has no staying power."

"You mean you're encouraging me? After last night, I thought…"

"I got to wondering about that. If anyone had told

me I was crazy to think Cary was the one, after just one date—"

"I know. You'd have been his pen pal from the Big House."

The two friends laughed, and Olivia felt better.

The adult volunteers, minus Morgana, broke for lunch, someone suggesting the temporary bistro set up next to the skating rink. After the morning's frenzy, they all needed sustenance—and a round of Irish coffees—before putting the rec center back in order. It was then, after the chairs had been stacked and the last of the glitter swept from the floor, that Olivia found the recorder with Jared's name on the back. Never mind that he'd left it behind in typical five-year-old fashion; she knew how much the instrument meant to him. She also knew that Gabriel was working and Morgana was on the town with the boys. Olivia would just drop the recorder at Walter's.

LEAVING THE INGREDIENTS for the night's ratatouille on his chopping bench, Gabriel raced home. Marmaduke had looked as if his patience was wearing thin with this latest interruption. Saturday night supper at the diner was always a big deal. But Morgana had called, hysterical, crying that Jared was sick and Walter was nowhere around.

Midafternoon, with a pale sun high in the sky, it was so cold the frosty air pricked his lungs as he ran, making him feel dizzy. He couldn't help thinking Monday and that bus to Oklahoma couldn't come fast enough. What was it Walter always said? Fish and guests smell after three days. Trouble was, technically Morgana wasn't a guest. And it looked as if—in one capacity or another—she was going to be in his and his sons' lives from now on. Their sons' lives. He just wished she could find the resolve to be more of a help than a hindrance.

He bounded up the porch steps to Walter's, only to find the front door unlocked and ajar. Morgana stood in the middle of the living room, one hand pressed to her mouth. "Oh, I just can't stand the smell of vomit," she wailed, frantically waving her other hand. "I feel like I'm going to be sick."

"Morgana, calm down." Olivia's voice came from the downstairs bathroom, where Justin hung about nervously at the door. "Think of the boys."

"Oh, Gabriel!" Morgana threw herself at him. "Thank God, you're here. I didn't know what to do. And of course it had to be Jared, and he won't talk, so it made everything so much more complicated."

Gabriel extricated himself from her clutches and went to Justin. "He's frowing up, Daddy, but he can't help it."

"I know, son." Gabriel stepped into the bathroom, to find Olivia gently holding Jared's head as he crouched over the toilet bowl.

"Have Morgana go to the corner store for ginger ale."

"We might have some."

"It'll give her something to do."

"Of course." Gabriel dug in his pocket for a five and almost pushed Morgana out on the porch with terse instructions to bring back a liter of ginger ale. Not Coca-Cola. Not root beer. Ginger ale.

Back in the bathroom, Olivia washed Jared's face as he sat on the floor. "He's going to be fine. Seems there was a little more than Christmas shopping going on."

"What do you mean?" Gabriel knelt in the doorway and pulled Justin onto his knee.

"What did you boys have to eat this afternoon?" Olivia asked, her words calm and kind.

"After rehearsal, we had lunch."

"At McDonald's?" Gabriel asked. Morgana didn't seem to understand how important he felt it was to limit the boys' intake of fast food.

"No. We bought candy bars at the drugstore. Morgana said they'd give us energy."

Gabriel bit back a curse.

"What else?" Olivia asked.

"After we bought Grampa a present, we got soft drinks from a machine."

"And what else?"

"Corn dogs from the gas station."

Gabriel was about to have a coronary. "Anything else?"

"Nachos. But Jared didn't look sick until after the doughnuts."

Gabriel ground his teeth. "That woman has less sense than a kid."

"Gabriel…" Looking a little green herself, Olivia shot him a warning glance. "Jared, honey, do you feel as if you're going to be sick again?"

He shook his head as he nestled against her.

She looked at Gabriel. "Believe me, I think he's empty. Do you have a hot water bottle?"

"My father has a heating pad he keeps by his La-Z-Boy. For his knee."

"No electrical cords for kids."

"Of course. My mother used to keep a hot water bottle in the upstairs linen closet."

"Let's go look for it," she said, rising and then lifting Jared into her arms. "We'll get this boy in bed with a hot water bottle to cuddle and some ginger ale to sip, and he'll be Spider-Man strong in no time. Won't you?"

With his head on her shoulder, Jared offered Gabriel and Justin a wan smile.

"Ms. Marshall knows what to do when someone frows up," Justin said, taking Gabriel's hand. "Kids do it all the time in school. Sometimes kids who aren't even in our class."

Gabriel smiled. The first time he'd done so in days.

At the top of the stairs, he and Justin looked through the linen closet and found the hot water bottle. It was old, but appeared to be in good shape.

"Put really hot water in it," Olivia called from the boys' room, "but wrap it in a towel."

Gabriel and Justin did as she instructed. The worried look was gone from Justin's face, and Gabriel had to admit Olivia's gentle efficiency was reassuring. This woman was the real deal, without an ounce of motive or manipulation. All the anger he'd felt after she'd told him of his mother's confession faded away.

By the time they brought the hot water bottle into the bedroom, Olivia had Jared in his pajamas and tucked in his bed. Suddenly, Gabriel saw his old room through Olivia's eyes. Especially the model airplanes hanging from the ceiling. It struck him that those models, constructed over one very long, hard winter, had been a project he and Walter had completed together. Just the two of them. Daniel hadn't had the patience. After all these years, Walter still hadn't thrown them out. In fact, they didn't have a speck of dust on them.

"I know you're getting ready for supper at the diner," she said. "So I'll stay with Morgana and the boys until Walter gets home."

"You'd do that?"

"Of course."

"We can read stories," Justin suggested, climbing up on his own bed and rummaging through the book-shelf at the head. "Ms. Marshall's a good reader."

Gabriel hesitated. He was the responsible party here. He should stay home.

"Go," Olivia urged. "We'll be fine." She said it with such conviction that the simple three-word statement seemed like a much bigger benediction. There weren't many people he truly trusted with his sons, but Olivia had become one of them.

He kissed both twins on the tops of their heads, then without thinking, kissed Olivia on the top of hers. Her eyes widened.

"We have to talk." He couldn't believe he'd said that. He was going to have to turn in his Official Man card.

On his way out he met Morgana coming in. "Take a little ginger ale up to Jared," he said. "No ice."

"You're not leaving me, are you, babe?"

In more ways than one.

JUST BEGINNING TO READ *Anansi and the Moss-Covered Rock,* Olivia heard the door close downstairs. Several minutes later Morgana appeared with a glass of ginger ale, which she set on the nightstand between the two beds. Silently, she slid to the floor and listened to the story.

Jared was asleep before the book's end, and Justin's eyes were drooping, too. With a finger to her lips, Olivia pulled the covers over Justin, then beckoned Morgana to follow her downstairs.

In the kitchen, Olivia put a kettle on for tea.

"I really screwed up, didn't I?" Morgana asked.

"Only if you didn't learn what to do the next time."

"Is Gabriel mad at me?"

"You'll have to ask him."

"Do you hate me?"

"No!" Olivia turned to look at the woman, who seemed more like a young child. "I want what's best for Justin and Jared. They need their mom."

"But you knew exactly what to do. I didn't."

"I've had a lot of experience with kids," Olivia explained, putting tea bags in mugs and setting the mugs on the table.

"So why don't you have any of your own?"

"I've never found the right guy."

Morgana's eyes widened in disbelief. "Never?"

"In college, I was engaged. But after graduation I had to move back here to take care of my aunt, and my fiancé thought that was a real bummer."

"Guys want you all to themselves."

"Some guys, it would seem."

"But there are some really nice men in Hennings. I've met a lot of them in just a week."

"And I've dated quite a few." Olivia poured hot water over the tea bags, then sat opposite Morgana.

"How come one of those guys hasn't snapped you up? I mean you're…pretty. And nice."

There was that awful four-letter word. "No chemistry, I guess."

"I don't know," Morgana said, staring into her tea. "I've never been able to afford to be picky. Gabriel was as close to a knight in shining armor as I'll ever come, but I think I've messed it up with him. I didn't have time to get him a present today. I don't even know what he'd like."

"He really does need a warm coat."

"So Justin said."

"Morgana, back to the kids. Parenthood takes practice. Just like most things in life. I get better as a teacher every year I teach. Gabriel gets better as a chef with each meal he cooks. And you…"

Morgana looked her right in the eye. "You don't know what I do, do you?"

"Not really."

"I'm an exotic dancer. In clubs. For men."

Okay, here was the chance to take the other woman down. But instead, Olivia took a deep breath and thought of Justin and Jared. "There's no reason an exotic dancer can't be a good mother."

"No wonder the boys love you."

It wasn't easy doing the right thing.

The front door opened. "I'm home!" Walter called out.

"You need to work this out with Gabriel," Olivia told Morgana. And to do that they didn't need any distractions or interference. Olivia stood up and poured her tea down the sink. "I'll just check on the boys once more, then I'll let you and Walter take it from here."

She passed Walter in the hall. In response to his puzzled look, she said, "Morgana will fill you in."

Upstairs, she looked in on the boys, who were sleeping peacefully, and although she knew she'd see them in school—as their teacher—this felt like goodbye. She allowed herself to kiss them each on the cheek. To smell their fusty little-boy scent. To listen to their even breathing. Despite their past troubles, they were lucky. They had Gabriel.

CHAPTER SEVENTEEN

AT SCHOOL ON MONDAY, Justin didn't mention the weekend incident, nor did he say whether Morgana would be leaving as planned. But after school, Walter was alone when he came to pick up the boys. He was unusually reticent.

On Tuesday afternoon, as she drove the bins of recycling materials her class had collected to the center just outside town, she saw Gabriel walking down Main Street in a warm new jacket. It appeared Morgana had given in to the suggestion.

On Wednesday, the last day of school before winter break, and a half day, the twins seemed to stick closer to her than usual. Before dismissal, she told them she'd see them on Saturday for the pageant performance, and told them to have a fun vacation.

"We wish it would snow," Justin replied, "so you could go sliding with us."

So did she.

Perhaps a lovely layer of white on the ground would cover the emptiness she felt.

Thursday evening, she went caroling with friends,

and felt the support that community could give. Trouble was, she craved something beyond ordinary friendship.

By Friday, she still hadn't heard from Gabriel, although she clearly remembered he'd said they needed to talk. She didn't get out of her pajamas all day.

On Saturday, the twenty-second, the first day of winter dawned bright and cold without a snowflake in sight. The pageant wasn't until seven that evening, but she had a million things to do to get ready before then. She couldn't allow herself to wallow in self-pity. She needed to pull herself up by her elf slippers and get on with her life.

By six o'clock, when the children began to assemble at the rec center and Olivia looked into their eager faces, she felt as if someone had sprinkled her with a little Christmas wonder. A little holiday magic. After all, children were what Christmas was all about. And then it hit her, right there as a parade of pint-size wooden soldiers passed. She could have a child, if that was what she really and truly wanted. As a single woman, she could adopt a child who needed her as much as she needed him. This budding idea was a Christmas present she'd give herself.

"Are you ready for this year's production?" Lynn asked, shuffling a stack of sheet music.

"Absolutely." In more ways than one. Aunt Lydia always used to say, *If life throws you lemons, play stickball.*

By six forty-five the rec center was standing room only. Olivia spotted Gabriel and Walter in the back. Marmaduke always closed the diner for the pageant, because every year it seemed as if his entire staff had some relative or another in the production. Amazingly, the sight of Gabriel in the audience didn't cause her pain—it gave her encouragement. For a successful performance tonight. As a girl, she'd always thought he was a person she'd want watching her back.

Break a leg, she told herself.

Gabriel stood in the audience and watched Olivia's every move. She seemed so in control, so self-contained. A little bit daunting, in fact. He'd said they needed to talk, but after putting Morgana on the bus, he'd taken all the hours at the diner Marmaduke could give him. Partly to make up for the time he'd taken off. Partly to earn a little extra for some Santa surprises, come Christmas morning. But mostly to give himself time to think of what, exactly, he wanted to talk to Olivia about.

"Hey, look at that," Walter said at his side as the lights above the audience dimmed. "Jared's first."

And there on the stage, amid a couple dozen other children clutching recorders, stood his son. Shoulders back, head high, a confident grin on his face. This was not the boy he'd brought to Hennings four and a half weeks ago. Tonight, it didn't matter that he didn't speak. He tootled with the best of them. And bowed afterward, as if he was born to be on the stage.

"I'll be!" Walter declared, clapping wildly. "I do believe he has your mother's talent!"

It took a minute for the full impact of that remark to sink in. Maybe Olivia was right. Maybe Gabriel needed to let the past go. To concentrate on the tenuous links he and the old man were beginning to forge because of Justin and Jared. Walter might have had doubts about Gabriel's paternity, but any misgivings sure had disappeared with the next generation of Brants.

Gabriel leaned against the back wall and let himself think about what it might be like to be a real part of Hennings. In this atmosphere, it wasn't hard. He clapped as the delicate snowflakes twirled, held his breath as an overexuberant dreidel careened too close to the background scenery, and laughed when Mrs. Frost produced some real ice cubes to stuff down Jack Frost's neck. Clearly an ad-lib.

When had he lost the ability to live life with a kid's bravado?

A loud bleating came from the building's entryway behind the audience, followed by some scuffling and nervous giggles. "He's eating my pants!" a small voice protested.

The piano began to play an intro, as miniature shepherds, their heads and bodies wrapped in towels fastened with assorted ropes, scarves and belts, began a slow march down the center aisle amid a motley crew of surprisingly well-behaved animals. Ty Mackey brought up the rear. At the front of the hall the group formed a semicircle, and the children sang "The Friendly Beasts," their sweet and clear soprano voices punctuated only occasionally by a pig's baritone squeal. The purity and the innocence of the moment made Gabriel's heart tighten. Wasn't this why he'd brought his boys home?

The rest of the program passed in a blur until the thunderous ovation at the end, when three young girls presented Olivia, the pianist and one other woman with bouquets of flowers. He thought of the two wrapped gifts Justin and Jared had insisted they bring to give Olivia after the performance. He didn't know what they were—Walter had helped wrap them—but they were tucked into one deep pocket of Gabriel's new coat. Another surprise. From Walter. An early Christmas present, he'd said, because watching Gabriel run around town in that flimsy windbreaker made the old man cold.

As children found their parents and the crowd began to thin, a new excitement built by the center's front doors.

"Snow!"

It looked as if Hennings was going to get its white Christmas, after all.

"Daddy, Grampa, did you like our songs?" Justin asked breathlessly as he and his brother materialized amid the sea of coats.

"It was wonderful," Walter replied, a catch in his throat.

"Can we give Ms. Marshall her presents?"

"Yes, but let's go together. I don't want to lose you." Gabriel turned to Walter. "Coming?"

"You go ahead," his father said with a misty-eyed wink at the boys. "I'll meet up with you at home. I'm going to start the hot chocolate."

Home. The word didn't sound so unnatural anymore.

As his sons clung to his coat, Gabriel made his way up the center aisle to the stage, where Olivia was giving Ty Mackey a hug. To Gabriel's mind, Ty didn't need to lean in quite so much. Nor thread his fingers in Olivia's hair. Nor close his eyes. It didn't help that instead of looking old and crusty as Noah, Ty was young and fit, with obvious good taste in women.

"Didn't the children do a terrific job!" Olivia exclaimed when she saw them, pulling away from Ty.

"Yup, we did," Justin agreed.

"The kids have something they want to give you," Gabriel said, sizing up the animal handler.

"Later, then," Ty countered. The squeeze he gave Olivia's shoulder seemed unnecessary.

Olivia came down from the stage to kneel next to the boys. "Now what's this about a gift?"

"Daddy?"

Gabriel pulled the two presents from his pocket. Justin took one and handed it to Olivia. "This one's from me."

Very carefully, she opened it. A penny dropped on the floor, leaving a coupon in her hand.

"It's for McDonald's," Justin said, picking up the penny and giving it back to her. "Grampa gave me the coupon, and I found the money in the desk in our room. Maybe when you go, we could go, too."

The look on Olivia's face was one of astonishment. "Did you know about this?" she asked, holding out the penny and staring up at Gabriel.

"No. The boys thought up the gifts on their own."

She turned the penny over. "You kept it."

It was the Indian Head penny she'd given him that summer so long ago. He'd forgotten all about it until this moment. His lucky penny, he'd called it, and he'd carried it everywhere as a kid. Maybe he should have taken it with him when he'd left Hennings seventeen years ago. Maybe things would have turned out differently.

"Was it wrong to give it to her, Daddy?" Justin asked. "You said we could have the stuff in your desk."

"No, it wasn't wrong. It's a terrific gift." It had been many years ago. It was now.

"Thank you!" Olivia smiled broadly at Justin, and then seemed to make herself busy tucking the coupon, the penny and the wrappings carefully into the pocket of her slacks.

Jared held out his hand to Gabriel for his gift, then passed it to Olivia. "More?" she said, her eyes bright. Jared nodded vigorously.

She slipped the ribbon off his present, which was a rolled piece of paper. "Oh, I hope this is a picture," she said. Jared couldn't contain his smile.

"It is!" she exclaimed. "And what a beautiful picture—so many colors!"

Gabriel saw a big, yellow smiley face sun looking down on a house with a porch and lots of pointy parts to the roof. There was a parrot in one of the windows. And on the emerald-green lawn were five stick figures, labeled in Walter's handwriting. Grampa, Justin, Jared, Daddy, Ms. Marshall.

Olivia's cheeks were tinged with pink. "We talked about titles in class, didn't we, Jared? Does this picture have a title?"

He nodded.

"Can you tell me what it is?"

He pulled on her sleeve so that she had to lean close, and then in a quiet, but distinct voice, a voice Gabriel hadn't heard in twenty-eight months, he said, "Family."

Gabriel thought his heart might stop beating.

"And family starts with the letter F," Justin said, as if his brother speaking was no big deal. "So did you like our presents, Ms. Marshall?"

She enveloped both boys in a big hug. "I love your presents!" she replied, with the same catch Walter had had in his throat.

"Olivia!" Lynn came up and handed her her coat. "We've decided to leave the cleanup till tomorrow morning.... Are you all right?"

"Yes," Olivia replied. "Exhausted, but deeply moved."

Lynn looked directly at Gabriel. "Would you see that she gets home?"

"Absolutely."

"Did anyone notice it's snowing?"

"Snow!" Justin cried, jumping up and down with Jared. "Let's go see."

"Wait for us," Gabriel cautioned, helping Olivia into her coat. The act felt proprietary. And good. Very good.

"Come on!" Justin and Jared looked as if they couldn't contain themselves. "Can we go sliding?"

"Maybe tomorrow," Olivia replied, laughing. "But tonight you can make snow angels on my front lawn."

Outside, the snow was coming down in big, fluffy clumps, the kind that seemed almost unreal. Olivia threw back her head, opened her mouth and stuck out her tongue to catch the flakes. The boys thought that was hilarious, but Gabriel found it painfully sensuous.

They crossed the street to the big Victorian, whose lovely old bones were strung with twinkling lights. The twins went wild, chasing each other on the front lawn in the newfallen snow. Olivia climbed the porch steps and sat on the top one. Gabriel sat down beside her. "Funny, how you don't have to show kids born and raised in the South what to do with snow," he said. They sat in silence, watching the boys' antics.

He felt her fingers on his arm. "That's a nice new coat," she said, her voice faintly wistful. "It looks warm."

"If this wasn't a gift out of the blue."

"How so?"

"Walter gave it to me last Sunday."

"Walter?"

"Yeah. Amid a lot of hemming and hawing, he said the damnedest thing. Said it was real good I put the boys first, but sometimes I needed to take care of myself. What do you think of that?"

"I think you wouldn't be reading too much into it if you said Walter was trying to tell you you've done well raising your sons."

"You think?"

"Yeah. That he's proud, even."

"Don't go overboard."

Justin and Jared came running up, panting. "Can we have hot chocolate?"

"I might have some instant cocoa inside," Olivia offered. Tentatively.

"Grampa's making hot chocolate at home," Gabriel said, trying not to be moved by the look of disappointment on Olivia's face. "Now, let me talk to Ms. Marshall a minute more."

The boys flew down the steps to tumble in a snowy heap on the lawn.

The adults stood.

"Olivia, I'd like to start over."

"What do you mean?"

"When I rolled into town before Thanksgiving, I was in such a lousy state of mind."

"And you're not now?"

"Let's see." He didn't know if he was crazy or

not, but it was worth a shot. "Pretend this is your classroom on that first day you met the boys." He stuck out his hand. "I'm Gabriel Brant. Do you remember me? Because I sure remember you."

She put her hand in his. "That summer."

"Yeah. Who could forget?" He turned toward his boys, who were trying to make snowballs. "Those are my sons, Justin and Jared. Although I'm not married. Are you?"

"No." She smiled shyly, and he could hardly bear how delicious she looked, sweet in the lamplight and frosted with snowflakes.

"Then, would you like to go out sometime? To catch up? Talk about old times?"

"I...I'd really like that."

"You free tomorrow night? Seven o'clock for dinner?"

"You work fast!"

"Not fast enough, believe me."

"Okay." She shook his hand, and he could feel the heat through her glove and his. "Tomorrow night, then. Seven o'clock. You know where I live."

"I think I can find my way back." He felt an enormous weight lift from the center of him. "Come on, boys," he shouted, bounding off the steps. "Let's go see if your grampa really did get the hot chocolate ready."

OLIVIA HAD NO IDEA what this dinner with Gabriel meant tonight. Was it a date? Was it the talk he'd said they needed to have? If so, what did he want to discuss? He'd said he wanted to start over, but what did that mean? And what about his mood? He'd been almost playful the night before, during their final exchange. What had gotten into him?

Whatever it was, it deserved more than her kindergarten "uniform"; more, even, than her weekend "sophisticated look." Tonight, if it really was a fresh start, it deserved some kick. She pulled from the back of her closet an impulse buy she'd never had the opportunity to wear. It was a wraparound dress in the softest wine-red wool, with a plunging neckline. It hugged all her curves and felt like a caress. When she stepped into four-inch heels she'd only ever worn around her bedroom, she had to admit she felt...dangerous.

The doorbell rang. Seven on the dot.

At the front door, Gabriel stood with a rakish grin and two grocery bags. "Wow," he breathed. "You look awesome. I don't know if it's safe to let me in. Not on the first date, anyway."

So her impulse buy was worth every penny. Trying not to blush, she indicated the grocery bags. "Are you running late?"

"No. These are for dinner."

"You're cooking?"

"Pattypan squash and shrimp. Did you think I'd trust this meal to anyone else?"

Oh, my. The after-dinner possibilities had just expanded.

"Well, are you going to let me in?"

She stepped aside. "I'd better put the sheet over Burt," she said, watching Gabriel stride down the hall to her kitchen as if he belonged there. Giving her house a whole different—exciting—feel. "I'll start a fire, too."

"Hold off on the fire," he called back. "I need you in here."

Now didn't that sound lovely?

"What shall I do?" she asked when she finally entered the kitchen. He was already chopping and sautéing, using utensils she hadn't even known she possessed.

He handed her a glass of white wine. "Keep me company."

Oh, yes.

But before she let herself go, she had to ask, "What about Morgana?"

He transferred lightly sautéed squash and shrimp to a buttered casserole dish, then looked directly at her. "Morgana's a given now. She wants to be part of the boys' lives. She did agree to give me custody, though. She'll get liberal visitation rights. Here in Hennings, until she settles down. If she ever does settle down."

"What about the two of you?"

"There is no two of us." He stopped what he was doing to look directly into Olivia's eyes. "I don't love her."

"You don't?"

"No. I think I love someone else."

"You think…"

"I think I need to put some effort into exploring that possibility." He glanced upward, to where a large clump of beribboned mistletoe hung from the light fixture. Now, where had that come from?

His lips on hers prevented her from further thoughts of mistletoe or Morgana or even pattypan shrimp. He kissed her as if he was in no hurry to do anything else. As if he might be sticking around. As if whatever they might start tonight could have a chance to blossom as the seasons changed.

He kissed her slowly. Deeply. Thoroughly. As if he was trying to show her everything he couldn't say.

Because what he said, when finally they broke apart, was, "I can't make promises. Not now. I still have too much uncertainty in my day-to-day life."

"Then let's take it day to day."

"You're a remarkable woman."

"But?"

"No buts. Although I feel selfish not being able to offer you what you deserve."

"Are you crazy? So far—and I'm going back a few years, mind you—you've offered friendship. And then…" she wound her arms around his neck "…you know." She kissed his throat. "Now, tonight, you're giving me food, glorious food. That I don't have to prepare. Tell me what more I should want on a minute-by-minute basis?"

"You're willing to go minute by minute?"

"Second by second."

"In that case…" He unwound her arms from his neck to put the casserole dish in the fridge. "Supper can wait."

As he led her out of the kitchen, she tried to peer into one of the grocery bags. "I hope there's something chocolate in there."

"There is. For after. Along with bacon and eggs. For breakfast."

EPILOGUE

ON THE SATURDAY AFTER the last day of school in June, Olivia relaxed in the shade on her cluttered front porch. She'd just finished hosting her annual cookies-and-punch party for her students and their parents. It had been a rousing success. Now, she leaned against an intricately carved porch post amid the colorful crepe streamers fluttering in the soft summer breeze, and thought of her students' unofficial graduation. Another group had moved on. A step away from her, a step closer to independence.

Usually, this was a melancholy moment. Not this year, however. Two of her students were still in her life. Justin and Jared.

Although some of her friends thought she was crazy to settle for a day-by-day relationship with Gabriel, Olivia didn't agree. Living in the moment was strangely liberating.

Of course, there had been a few difficulties. Justin and Jared had had to learn that at school there was a public Ms. Marshall and at home a private "Livvy." The board of education had had to learn—

when Adrienne Quincy had pulled Robert out of Olivia's class with a scathing letter detailing why— that a contract was a contract. And that Olivia had, in dating Gabriel, in no way compromised hers. Olivia had learned that she was entitled to her wants, as well as her needs.

With a smile, she began picking up party plates and napkins.

"Hey."

She spun around to find Gabriel staring at her from the steps. "I thought you were due at the diner right after the party."

"Marmaduke sent me away."

"He fired you? Oh, let me at him."

"Hold on! There was no firing. He has a proposition for me."

"What kind of proposition?" Watching the breeze ruffle his dark hair, Olivia could think of several propositions she'd like to offer.

Gabriel pulled her down on the top step of the porch. The bees buzzed in the garden, which was just beginning to flower. "Marmaduke wants to retire. To North Carolina to be near his daughter and grandchildren. He says he can handle his rental properties long distance, but not the diner."

"And?"

"He wanted to know if I'd be interested in managing it."

Olivia felt disappointment for Gabriel. She knew his goal was to have his own restaurant again one day. Managing for Marmaduke would still be working for someone else.

He slipped his arm around her shoulder. "Why the long face?"

"Is this what you want?"

"Listen to the whole deal." Gabriel grew visibly excited. "I'd manage for a year. The menu, the whole operation would be up to me. If, after the year, I see the diner as something I could put my own stamp on, Marmaduke would turn it over to me. Would hold the mortgage. It would be my restaurant."

"Oh, Gabriel!" Joyfully, she threw herself into his arms, but felt him stiffen. "What's wrong?"

"It seems perfect on the surface, but…"

"Is it Hennings? Are you aiming bigger?" The thought of Gabriel and the boys leaving nearly broke her heart. It certainly shattered her live-in-the-moment equilibrium.

"There's only one missing piece. One really big unanswered question."

This didn't sound good. She fingered the lucky Indian Head penny, which she'd had made into a pendant.

"Maybe you can help me work through it."

"Of course."

He stood, then began to pace, worry lines creasing his forehead.

This didn't look good. She stood, too, but clung to the porch railing until her knuckles whitened. "Gabriel, please, how difficult can it be?"

He stopped in front of her, his frown replaced by a boyish grin. "Do you remember back at Christmas I said I thought I loved someone?"

She nodded. How could she have forgotten? Although he'd never mentioned it again, she'd kept the memory always with her, as she had the penny.

"I love you, Olivia. Will you marry me?"

"Marriage?" She was stunned. She'd almost convinced herself he wasn't the marrying kind.

"Don't keep me in suspense," he pleaded. "How does our story end?"

She let herself breathe. "Happily ever after, of course. Yes, I'll marry you!" she exclaimed, as he took her in his arms and spun her around the porch.

She already knew the ceremony would take place in the backyard under the maple. Where it had all begun. And she couldn't help thinking ahead to next Christmas, when this old house would be, as Walter liked to say, "bustin' at the seams." With holiday decorations. With hidden presents. With get-togethers and good food.

With family.

* * * * *

SPECIAL EDITION®

LIFE, LOVE AND FAMILY

*These contemporary romances will strike
a chord with you as heroines juggle life
and relationships on their way to true love.*

New York Times *bestselling author*
Linda Lael Miller
*brings you a BRAND-NEW contemporary story
featuring her fan-favorite McKettrick family.*

Meg McKettrick is surprised to be reunited
with her high school flame, Brad O'Ballivan.
After enjoying a career as a country-and-
western singer, Brad aches for a home and
family…and seeing Meg again makes him
realize he still loves her. But their pride
manages to interfere with love…until an unexpected matchmaker gets involved.

Turn the page for a sneak preview of
THE McKETTRICK WAY
by Linda Lael Miller
On sale November 20, wherever books are sold.

Brad shoved the truck into gear and drove to the bottom of the hill, where the road forked. Turn left, and he'd be home in five minutes. Turn right, and he was headed for Indian Rock.

He had no damn business going to Indian Rock.

He had nothing to say to Meg McKettrick, and if he never set eyes on the woman again, it would be two weeks too soon.

He turned right.

He couldn't have said why.

He just drove straight to the Dixie Dog Drive-In.

Back in the day, he and Meg used to meet at the Dixie Dog, by tacit agreement, when either of them had been away. It had been some kind of universe thing, purely intuitive.

Passing familiar landmarks, Brad told himself he ought to turn around. The old days were gone. Things had ended badly between him and Meg anyhow, and she wasn't going to be at the Dixie Dog.

He kept driving.

He rounded a bend, and there was the Dixie Dog. Its big neon sign, a giant hot dog, was all lit up and going through its corny sequence—first it was covered in red squiggles of light, meant to suggest ketchup, and then yellow, for mustard.

Brad pulled into one of the slots next to a speaker, rolled down the truck window and ordered.

A girl roller-skated out with the order about five minutes later.

When she wheeled up to the driver's window, smiling, her eyes went wide with recognition, and she dropped the tray with a clatter.

Silently Brad swore. Damn if he hadn't forgotten he was a famous country singer.

The girl, a skinny thing wearing too much eye makeup, immediately started to cry. "I'm sorry!" she sobbed, squatting to gather up the mess.

"It's okay," Brad answered quietly, leaning to look down at her, catching a glimpse of her plastic name tag. "It's okay, Mandy. No harm done."

"I'll get you another dog and a shake right away, Mr. O'Ballivan!"

"Mandy?"

She stared up at him pitifully, sniffling. Thanks to the copious tears, most of the goop on her eyes had slid south. "Yes?"

"When you go back inside, could you not mention seeing me?"

"But you're Brad O'Ballivan!"

"Yeah," he answered, suppressing a sigh. "I know."

She rolled a little closer. "You wouldn't happen to have a picture you could autograph for me, would you?"

"Not with me," Brad answered.

"You could sign this napkin, though," Mandy said. "It's only got a little chocolate on the corner."

Brad took the paper napkin and her order pen, and scrawled his name. Handed both items back through the window.

She turned and whizzed back toward the side entrance to the Dixie Dog.

Brad waited, marveling that he hadn't considered incidents like this one before he'd decided to come back home. In retrospect, it seemed short-sighted, to say the least, but the truth was, he'd expected to be—Brad O'Ballivan.

Presently Mandy skated back out again, and this time she managed to hold on to the tray.

"I didn't tell a soul!" she whispered. "But Heather and Darlene *both* asked me why my mascara was all smeared." Efficiently she hooked the tray onto the bottom edge of the window.

Brad extended payment, but Mandy shook her head.

"The boss said it's on the house, since I dumped your first order on the ground."

He smiled. "Okay, then. Thanks."

Mandy retreated, and Brad was just reaching for the food when a bright red Blazer whipped into the space beside his. The driver's door sprang open, crashing into the metal speaker, and somebody got out in a hurry.

Something quickened inside Brad.

And in the next moment Meg McKettrick was standing practically on his running board, her blue eyes blazing.

Brad grinned. "I guess you're not over me after all," he said.

▼ *Silhouette*®

SPECIAL EDITION™

**brings you a heartwarming
new McKettrick's story from**

NEW YORK TIMES BESTSELLING AUTHOR

LINDA LAEL MILLER

THE McKETTRICK
Way

Meg McKettrick is surprised to be reunited
with her high school flame, Brad O'Ballivan,
who has returned home to his family's
neighboring ranch. After seeing Meg again,
Brad realizes he still loves her. But the pride
of both manage to interfere with love...until
an unexpected matchmaker gets involved.

—— McKettrick Women ——

Available December wherever you buy books.

Visit Silhouette Books at www.eHarlequin.com SSEIBC24867

THE ITALIAN BILLIONAIRE'S CHRISTMAS MIRACLE
by *Catherine Spencer*
Book #: 2688

Domenico Silvaggio d'Avalos knows that beautiful,
unworldly Arlene Russell isn't mistress material—
but might she be suitable as his wife?

HIS CHRISTMAS BRIDE
by *Helen Brooks*
Book #: 2689

Powerful billionaire Zak Hamilton understood
Blossom's vulnerabilities, and he had to have her.
What was more, he'd make sure he claimed her
as his bride—by Christmas!

Be sure not to miss out on these two fabulous
Christmas stories available December 2007,
brought to you by Harlequin Presents!

www.eHarlequin.com

HPCM1207

Introducing

a brand-new miniseries with light-hearted
and playful stories that will make you Blush...
because who says that sex has to be serious?

Starting in December with...

BABY, IT'S COLD OUTSIDE
by Cathy Yardley

Chilly temperatures send Colin Reeves and
Emily Stanfield indoors—then it's sparks, sensual
heat and hot times ahead! But will their private
holiday hometown reunion last longer than
forty-eight delicious hours in bed?

www.eHarlequin.com

HB79370

REQUEST YOUR FREE BOOKS!
2 FREE NOVELS PLUS 2 FREE GIFTS!

HARLEQUIN®

Super Romance®

Exciting, emotional, unexpected!

YES! Please send me 2 FREE Harlequin Superromance® novels and my 2 FREE gifts. After receiving them, if I don't wish to receive any more books, I can return the shipping statement marked "cancel." If I don't cancel, I will receive 6 brand-new novels every month and be billed just $4.69 per book in the U.S., or $5.24 per book in Canada, plus 25¢ shipping and handling per book and applicable taxes, if any*. That's a savings of close to 15% off the cover price! I understand that accepting the 2 free books and gifts places me under no obligation to buy anything. I can always return a shipment and cancel at any time. Even if I never buy another book from Harlequin, the two free books and gifts are mine to keep forever.   135 HDN EEX7   336 HDN EEYK

Name	(PLEASE PRINT)	
Address		Apt.
City	State/Prov.	Zip/Postal Code

Signature (if under 18, a parent or guardian must sign)

Mail to the **Harlequin Reader Service**®:
IN U.S.A.: P.O. Box 1867, Buffalo, NY 14240-1867
IN CANADA: P.O. Box 609, Fort Erie, Ontario L2A 5X3

Not valid to current Harlequin Superromance subscribers.

Want to try two free books from another line?
Call 1-800-873-8635 or visit www.morefreebooks.com.

* Terms and prices subject to change without notice. NY residents add applicable sales tax. Canadian residents will be charged applicable provincial taxes and GST. This offer is limited to one order per household. All orders subject to approval. Credit or debit balances in a customer's account(s) may be offset by any other outstanding balance owed by or to the customer. Please allow 4 to 6 weeks for delivery.

Your Privacy: Harlequin is committed to protecting your privacy. Our Privacy Policy is available online at www.eHarlequin.com or upon request from the Reader Service. From time to time we make our lists of customers available to reputable firms who may have a product or service of interest to you. If you would prefer we not share your name and address, please check here. ☐

HSR

Inside ROMANCE

Stay up-to-date on all your romance reading news!

Inside Romance is a FREE quarterly newsletter
highlighting our upcoming series releases
and promotions.

Visit

www.eHarlequin.com/InsideRomance

to sign up to receive our complimentary newsletter today!

IRN1107

Get ready to meet

THREE WISE WOMEN

with stories by

DONNA BIRDSELL,
LISA CHILDS

and

SUSAN CROSBY.

Don't miss these three unforgettable stories
about modern-day women and the love
and new lives they find on Christmas.

Look for *Three Wise Women*
Available December wherever you buy books.

HARLEQUIN®
NeXt™

TheNextNovel.com

HN88147

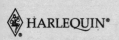

HARLEQUIN®

American ★ Romance®

Kate Merrill had grown up convinced
that the most attractive men were incapable
of ever settling down. Yet the harder she
resisted the superstar photographer
Tyler Nichols, the more persistent the
handsome world traveler became.
So by the time Christmas arrived, there
was only one wish on her holiday list—
that she was wrong!

LOOK FOR

THE CHRISTMAS DATE

BY

Michele Dunaway

**Available December
wherever you buy books**

www.eHarlequin.com   HAR75195

COMING NEXT MONTH